MORE THAN MEETS THE EYE

HOME FRONT HEROINES: USAF

CARRIE DAWS

IMMEASURABLE
WORKS

Identifiers: ISBN 978-1-947539-08-2 (paperback) | eISBN 978-1-947539-07-5 (ebook) | ISBN 978-1-947539-31-0 (large print hardcover)

1. Christian fiction—contemporary. 2. Christian fiction—inspirational families.

Unless otherwise indicated, Scriptures are taken from THE HOLY BIBLE, NEW INTERNATIONAL VERSION. Copyright 1973, 1978, 1984, 2011 by Biblica, Inc. Used by permission. All rights reserved worldwide.

Scripture taken from *THE MESSAGE*. Copyright 1993, 1994, 1995, 1996, 2000, 2001, 2002. Used by permission of NavPress Publishing Group.

Fonts used by permission of Microsoft Word

Cover design by Jarmal Wilcox

Page Layout by Carrie Daws

Published by Immeasurable Works, 104 Harvest Ln., Raeford, NC 28376, USA

We're not giving up. How could we! Even though on the outside it often looks like things are falling apart on us, on the inside, where God is making new life, not a day goes by without his unfolding grace. These hard times are small potatoes compared to the coming good times, the lavish celebration prepared for us. There's far more here than meets the eye. The things we see now are here today, gone tomorrow. But the things we can't see now will last forever.

2 Corinthians 4:16–18, The Message

PROLOGUE

September 2001, Anchorage, Alaska

"YOU TWO NEED TO SEE THIS."

Lori Braxton's brain struggled to process the blunt interruption to her sleep. She and her husband, Jonathan, a senior airman in the United States Air Force, had gone to bed late in a friend's spare bedroom. Yesterday had been spent cleaning the house on Elmendorf Air Force Base that they'd called home for the last seventeen months. Everything they owned was either on a ship heading for their new duty station at Malmstrom Air Force Base, Montana, or packed tightly in a small flatbed trailer her husband had added plywood walls and a roof to just two weeks prior. They were ready to sign out of housing, sign off the base, and head to the lower forty-eight.

Her friend appeared at their door again, but not as quietly as before. "Come on. It's important."

This time the urgency slammed into Lori's brain. "What time is it?" she mumbled, rubbing her eyes.

Her husband, Jonathan, shifted beside her. "It's 6:13."

Groaning, she stood up and shook out her pajama pants, unfolding the bottom cuff of one leg. Cautiously she stepped over four-year-old Kay sleeping peacefully on the floor through the disturbance. After covering two-year-old Charlie with his blanket, Lori ran her hands through her medium-length, hickory brown hair. Wondering what was up, she walked across the small upstairs landing to her friend's bedroom. The light from the television assaulted her eyes, the sound just barely loud enough to hear.

Lori yawned. "What's so important at six o'clock in the morning?"

"Pastor called," her friend said without taking her eyes off the TV. "Friends in Virginia woke him with the news, and he knew we'd want to know."

Strange was an understatement for this behavior. The hour alone was enough to cause concern for her normally late-sleeping friend, but the lack of eye contact and the drone of news on the television peaked Lori's interest. She stepped farther into the room, turning so she could see the screen. A lone skyscraper dominated the landscape, dark smoke billowing out from its top, lighter gray smoke rising from the ground.

Lori knelt on the floor near the television. "What is that?"

"New York City," her friend replied. "Two planes flew into the World Trade Center."

Lori struggled to process what she was seeing. "World Trade Center? But aren't there two skyscrapers?"

Her friend barely moved her head from side to side. "Not any more."

Jonathan appeared in the doorframe, his closely trimmed dark hair still disheveled from sleep. "What's going on?"

"The first tower fell just as I turned on the TV," her friend said.

Jonathan walked over to stand behind Lori. "You said planes did that? Like kamikazes?"

"Like United Airlines passenger planes," came the quiet reply.

Lori shook her head in disbelief. The rest of America had likely been glued to the news reports for hours while they had peacefully slept, unaware of the chaos happening on the east coast. Two planes full of people going about their normal lives had been taken over and forced into two buildings full of people going about their normal lives. "God help us," she whispered.

"There's more," their friend said.

Lori met her eyes, not sure she wanted to hear it. "A third plane hit the Pentagon. The Federal Aviation Administration has grounded all flights."

Lori gasped. "All flights? Nationwide?"

Her friend nodded. "All fifty states. And someone on the news right before I woke you suggested they might close the borders until they get a better handle on this thing."

Lori's mind swirled. They were supposed to drive out in three days, crossing the border into Canada and then again into Montana. Would Canada let them in? And if they did, would the United States allow them re-entry? And if they were trapped here, what would they do with all their household goods in crates on a ship headed to Seattle?

Jonathan touched her shoulder. "Come on, get the kids up. We've got to get to the base. The Shirt knows we're signing out of housing today, but he doesn't know how to reach us here."

Lori's mind raced. The Shirt was charged with keeping up with all his troops and dealing with any personnel issues. Surely, he would be one of the first to know if their orders to move had been canceled.

"I've got to check in," Jonathan continued. "It's probably

too soon after the attacks, but I have to see if they know what's going to happen with me."

Lori took a deep breath before standing. Military installations around the world would be on high alert, but civilian casualties took security to a new level. Their whole world, the life Americans had known, had just changed forever.

ONE

THIRTY-SIX DAYS. Six thousand two hundred miles. When they'd left Alaska on September fourteenth, no one in Jonathan's chain of command knew if they'd be able to cross into Canada or if they'd be able to cross back into the United States. Truthfully, no one knew much of anything other than al-Qaeda had successfully launched an attack on American soil, thousands had died, and PCS orders moving military families from one place to another had not been halted.

So, with orders and original birth certificates in hand, Jonathan and Lori had said goodbye to friends and headed north out of Anchorage on the Glenn Highway. Thankfully, crossing both borders had been simpler than they expected, and they'd visited family in Kentucky and Ohio before heading back west to sign in at Malmstrom Air Force Base near Great Falls, Montana.

"Boxes 154, 162, and 78."

Lori flipped through the pages of inventory the packers in Alaska had handed her. "Got it," she said and checked off the three box numbers per the mover's instructions. She watched him push the loaded dolly over to the corner of her new living room and add them to the pile already waiting for her.

A second man came through the front door hauling a plastic toddler bed with a small pink and blue house for the headboard. "First room on the right," she called out while scanning the list for the bed.

The first man was quickly through the door again with another load of boxes. "These are all labeled toys. Numbers 64, 67, 72, and..."

Lori waited as he checked the box over for a number. He finally shrugged and set it off to the side. "If you'll open it up to see what's in there, we'll leave it for last to see what's missing from the checklist."

"Okay," said Lori, checking the three numbers off. She grabbed the knife from her pocket. "The rest of those go in the basement."

Lori crouched down and sliced open the tape just as the second mover walked through the door.

"Here are 197, 198, and 203. Looks like crib pieces."

Lori checked the numbers off her list, calling out, "First room on the left." She turned her attention back to the box just before Kay surprised her by jumping onto her back.

"Momma! He, that mover man guy, he brought us our toys!"

Lori shifted slightly, catching her balance before Kay knocked them both over on the floor. "Kay, honey, where's your brother?"

"He's waiting downstairs, Momma. I told him to wait. I told him I'd come ask you to open our toys for us."

Lori gently grabbed Kay's arm, pulling her to stand beside her so she could look in her daughter's eyes. Lori's biggest problem with this house was the painted wooden stairs that ended on a solid concrete floor. Visions of her children sprawled and bleeding haunted her. "Didn't I tell you that I needed you to stay with your brother? To keep him safe, away from the stairs and out of the men's way?"

Kay nodded before pushing her straight, dark blonde hair out of her eyes. "But our toys will help us stay safe. They will," she said, her eyes wide and earnest. "We'll keep them over in the corner with the blanket you put down for us."

"Here's 274 and 249."

Lori picked up her checklist and marked the two boxes. "Got them," she called out. Turning her attention back to Kay, she smiled at her young daughter. "I can't come downstairs right now and open the boxes for you, but I just found something that will help you and Charlie have some fun."

"You did?" Kay's expression was a mix of hope and excitement. She clasped her hands together under her chin. "What is it? What did you find?"

Lori opened the lid of the unmarked box wider so Kay could see. It held one of their prized sets of building blocks along with a few of their smaller stuffed animals. Kay whooped in excitement.

"Go on," Lori said. "Take the animals and tell your brother that I'll bring the blocks down as soon as I mark off this next load of boxes the movers are bringing in for us."

———

WHEN THEY'D FIRST SIGNED on base, choosing their house had been an easy decision, but now Lori had her doubts.

Not that she thought a different decision would have been more realistic.

The housing officer had presented them with two choices for enlisted housing: an older unit which was slated for remodel within the next three years, or a newer unit that came with a waiting list. In other words, plan to most likely move within three years or find an apartment off base for nine-months and then definitely move. But, this being their fourth move in three years, it wasn't like moving was unfamiliar. Considering they still owned a house in Ohio that wouldn't sell, Jonathan and Lori were in agreement that they needed cheap housing fast. The older unit fit the bill, even if it wasn't the best house for their family.

"Now before I can hand you the keys," the lodging counselor had said when they'd signed to accept the house, "you have to sign this waiver. Tests confirm the house has lead paint, but as long as it doesn't chip and the kids don't eat it, you'll be fine."

Now, as Lori watched her kids playing around the boxes spread across the basement, she looked for painted surfaces around them. Kay was old enough that eating paint shouldn't be a problem, but with an active two-year-old and a third baby on the way, she'd asked for more specifics. Specifics the counselor didn't have to give her.

"I'm sorry," she'd said. "All the information I have is that it is in the basement, and it has been painted over, probably multiple times by now."

"But the basement is unfinished?" said Jonathan.

"Yes. The walls are concrete block that has been sealed, and it's a cement floor. The ceiling is open to the subfloor from the main level. Your washer and dryer hookups are down there, and I believe your water heater. But otherwise it's just open space most people use for storage."

Jonathan had looked at Lori for confirmation, and she appreciated that he didn't sign without her consent. She'd acquiesced, nodding her head and feeling trapped in a maze of bad choices between unknown dangers to her children and apartment rents they couldn't afford. *God, please protect my children*, she had prayed then and was praying again now as she stood among the giggling children and rows of boxes.

"Momma!" yelled Kay excitedly from behind her. "What's in this box?"

Lori sighed from exhaustion. Yesterday after the packers had finished unloading their crates, she'd managed to find sheets for their beds and a blanket for her and Jonathan to share. The kids had used the blankets they'd carried with them on the drive to Montana. Today she was hoping to get the kitchen in some semblance of order, but she had to get Kay and Charlie settled with a few more toys before they would let her focus elsewhere. The excitement of belongings they hadn't seen in two months was getting the better of all of them.

The support poles were the only possible source of lead paint in the basement, so surely she wasn't making a mistake allowing the kids to set up a play area down here. She nibbled on her lip as she considered her alternatives. With the possibility of Jonathan working shift work, she needed a place for the kids to play away from his sleeping area, but the small ranch house with bare wood floors echoed every sound. They couldn't afford to go buy multiple large area rugs to stifle the sound, so the basement seemed logical.

"Momma! This one!" yelled Kay again.

"Sorry, sweetie." Lori walked over, pulling a knife from her pocket. "It says *toys*. How about we open it to see what treasure lies inside, huh?"

"Yes!" yelled Kay, jumping in her excitement. "Come on, Charlie. Momma's gonna open a box for us."

JONATHAN BRAXTON SCRIBBLED his signature at the bottom of the post deployment health assessment, trying not to think too much about his health concerns. He tried to convince himself that he was just stressed. His ever-increasing battle with insomnia weighed heavily on his mind, but he couldn't figure out how it could be related to his time in Saudi, even though it had started after his first deployment there in the spring of 2000. He'd worked mostly nights both times he was assigned to Prince Sultan Air Base, but he'd returned stateside from the second trip over three months ago and had been on either day shift or leave. Switching his sleep schedule back to a normal routine shouldn't be the problem.

Moving on to the next page of the forms the young airman had handed him, he filled in the basic information for his initial PRP assessment. A doctor would have to sign off on it, but the Personnel Reliability Program now controlled his future as much as the Department of Defense did. Following his instructions, he read through the printed official directive governing his career, or at least the next three years of it.

"In accordance with Presidential Policy Directive 35 and DoDD 3150.02, nuclear weapon systems require special consideration because of their political and military importance, their destructive power, and the potential consequences of an accident or unauthorized act. Assured nuclear weapons safety, security, and control remain of paramount importance."

Jonathan skimmed down a little, already convinced of his duty to the United States and the importance of protecting its nuclear program.

"Only certified personnel will be assigned to U.S. nuclear weapons. Certification is based on informed decisions concerning an individual's reliability as determined through comprehensive screening and continuing evaluation. Disqualification or decertification of nuclear weapons personnel reliability assurance eligibility is neither a punitive measure nor the basis for disciplinary action. The failure of an individual to be qualified or certified does not necessarily reflect unfavorably on the individual's suitability for assignment to other, non-nuclear duties."

The page went on outlining the criteria that Jonathan had already met before accepting the assignment, this appointment today being near the end of the stringent checklist. Medical evaluation, personnel file review, and a personal interview were all that stood between him and his new duties protecting America's nuclear assets.

Which circled him right back to his concerns with his post deployment assessment. Stress could remove his eligibility. As could insomnia and every medication used to treat sleeping problems. And what exactly was he, a member of the Security Forces assigned to a base whose entire mission centered on the security of nuclear missiles, supposed to do if he couldn't be around those weapons?

No, he had to pass his assessments. When the doctor walked in, he would downplay his insomnia.

CHARLIE LAY AGAINST THE STARK white flat sheet covering the stiff bed at the base emergency clinic. He was perking up a little but was still too calm for Lori's comfort. This was not the best introduction to the base medical community, but Charlie's growing lethargy throughout the morning caused her great concern. He'd finished breathing in the liquid albuterol they'd added to his oxygen mask twenty-two minutes earlier, so she'd been watching for the medic who had just entered their little cubby.

"Let's take a look again, buddy," the airman said. He fastened the small instrument around Charlie's left index finger to measure his oxygen saturation level and waited patiently, watching the numbers flip between ninety-three and ninety-four. "Well, that's a bit better than the eighty-nine we saw when you first got here."

"Yes," said Lori, still trying to learn what these numbers meant for her son.

The medic listened to Charlie's chest for a minute. "Okay. Can you roll over for me, buddy? Onto your belly?"

Lori stood to help Charlie turn over, and the medic straightened out the shirt across his back. He cupped his hands slightly then began gently striking Charlie on his upper back, almost like he was using Charlie for a drum. "This can help break up the congestion inside his lungs," he explained, "and sometimes it will encourage the younger ones like your son to start coughing. Coughing is good. It can break up the congestion and help open all the airways in the lungs."

Lori nodded her head like she fully understood, but she didn't. How did congestion get into Charlie's lungs? And how did she keep it out?

"Mrs. Braxton?" The man in green scrubs who had just come around the curtain looked up from the chart in his hand. "I'm Doctor Warren. How's your son doing now?"

"He's better," Lori offered, glancing at the medic who was still tapping on Charlie's back.

"His O2 is up to ninety-four," the medic offered as Charlie coughed a couple of times.

"Good. Let's get him sitting up."

Charlie coughed a few more times as the medic lifted him back into a sitting position on the bed.

"Those are good, productive coughs," said Dr. Warren. "Exactly what we want to hear." He applied his stethoscope to Charlie's chest for a moment before looking back at Lori. "You said he had pneumonia?"

Lori nodded. "Yes. About six months ago."

"Was he hospitalized?"

"No. My husband was deployed, and I was home alone with both our children. I had to take him in to see the doctor every day, and she kept us on a strict medicine schedule for two weeks, but she allowed us to stay at home so I didn't have to find care for our daughter."

"I see. And he made a full recovery?"

"Yes. We haven't had any trouble all summer."

"Good." Dr. Warren made some notes on the chart. "Well, you can expect that this winter will present some challenges for you. Charlie's lungs are weak from the pneumonia, so he may have several episodes like this, especially with the cooler weather and all the colds that naturally circulate this time of year. I'm prescribing some albuterol for you to take home with you. Whenever you hear him wheezing—that rattled breathing like when you first came in—then just give him a dose at home and call his pediatrician. Do you have any questions for me?"

"So this is entirely related to his pneumonia? It couldn't be anything else?"

"Anything else? Like what?"

Lori rubbed Charlie's head. "Well, we had to sign a lead paint waiver when we signed into our house."

"Ah, yes. You're in the older housing inside the Second Street gate?"

Lori nodded, hoping the doctor would offer something to ease her mind.

"Your son's condition is definitely not related to lead poisoning. Lead doesn't affect the lungs or cause any breathing complications. For that you'll want to be watching for headaches, stomach cramps, irritability, trouble sleeping, those kinds of things."

"Okay." Lori was relieved but still overwhelmed as she thought through the doctors words. Wheezing? Several episodes this winter? Albuterol to take home? She didn't really understand what the doctor expected of her as it related to Charlie's breathing, but she couldn't formulate a coherent thought to begin asking questions.

"No other questions, then?" Dr. Warren seemed to take her silence as understanding, and he looked back toward the medic. "Make sure the release orders have them follow up with their doctor."

"Yes, sir." The medic turned back toward Charlie. "Well, young man, let's get you out of here for tonight."

Release orders. That sounded good. Maybe this wasn't as bad as she'd first thought. Of course, tomorrow she'd have to figure out how to make an appointment with whoever the new doctor was going to be.

―――――――

LORI HAD TROUBLE KEEPING her gaze off the clock. It was almost time for Jonathan to be home, and shortly after dinner, friends Reese and Joy Morgan would be arriving. She was anxious to see them, but even more excited to see Socks, the husky mix that Jonathan and Lori had adopted from the animal shelter on Charlie's first birthday.

Joy was active duty with just two years left until retirement. They'd wanted to stay in Anchorage where they had all been stationed together, but the Air Force wouldn't extend their time at Elmendorf AFB that long. So, they'd moved to Ellsworth AFB, South Dakota, a month before Jonathan and Lori had started for Montana. As they'd been able to get into housing quickly, they'd kept Socks while Jonathan processed into Malmstrom and got assigned housing.

Befriending Joy had been a considerable step outside of Lori's comfort zone. She and Jonathan had needed money to help cover the mortgage of the house in Ohio, so she'd signed up to do home day care on base. At the time, Joy had been in her last weeks of pregnancy with their third child, so Lori approached her one Sunday morning at church.

"I'm wondering if you'll be looking for a day care for your baby."

"Well," said Joy, struggling to get up out of a folding chair placed neatly in rows in their Sunday school classroom, "Reese and I have talked about it some and were considering it. My mom lives with us, but she has some health issues and probably shouldn't be lifting the baby."

Lori tucked a lock of hair behind her ear. "Well, I'm going through the classes required by the base to open a home day care. Would you consider letting me take care of—do you know if the baby is a boy or a girl?"

Joy's eyes lit up. Lori was always amazed how the woman exuded happiness when she smiled. Peace too. Joy just had a calming presence that made it seem like stress just rolled off of her without leaving any residue.

"We're having another girl," said Joy. "I'll have to talk to Reese, of course, but you keeping her during the day might work out really well."

And it had. For the fourteen remaining months Reese and Joy had been stationed at Elmendorf, baby Emily had become a large part of Lori's home and Charlie's best friend. Now, they were eight hours apart on the map but still a huge part of each other's lives.

Lori sighed deeply and turned from looking out the kitchen window. Neither watching the clock nor the driveway would bring her friends to her front door a moment sooner.

To try to pass the time, she went downstairs to survey where Joy and her family would sleep. Kay and Charlie were off in the far corner with their toys, running around in bare feet as usual, oblivious to the cold concrete floor. Was that good for Charlie's breathing? Should she insist he wear socks? At least he was acting more normal today, and the kids had a rug underneath most of the play area.

The trip across the Rockies had been hard with two little ones, an active dog, and a fully-loaded trailer dragging down their gas mileage, but when the Finance Office had calculated what the Air Force owed Jonathan for completing a partial DITY—or Do-It-Yourself—move, it had been worth every penny. Between that pay and a good sale, they'd been able to buy a living room set and three small area rugs, all set up in time for their first guests' arrival. Not quite everything they needed for the house, but it was more than she'd hoped for. Why couldn't someone at least demand standard-sized windows for military housing so the curtains would fit from one installation to the next?

Lori straightened the blanket covering their only air mattress, already blown up and sitting on the rug by the couches for Reese and Joy. Clearly one or both of her kids had crawled across it once or twice. Joy's two older kids could each have a couch to sleep on, which only left little Emily, who would most likely want to sleep with Kay and Charlie.

A door slammed upstairs, and Lori heard heavy footsteps. "Daddy's home," she called to the kids. They rushed for the stairs, and she followed behind, watching for signs that one of them was tripping or falling. She didn't know if she'd ever shake her imaginations of blood-covered concrete that tensed her muscles every time her babies decided to go up or down the painted wood steps, and for the hundredth time she considered moving the play area upstairs.

Charlie managed the final stair on his hands and knees before standing to rush to where Kay clung to Jonathan's leg. Jonathan scooped Charlie up in a bear hug, snuggling in to nibble on his neck. Lori leaned against the doorframe, soaking in the kids' giggles and Jonathan's smiles. How she loved these moments!

Jonathan shifted Charlie onto his hip before looking at his wife. "I got my assignment today."

He'd prepared her for this at the beginning of the week. Once he finished in processing and the final PRP evaluations, he'd find out where his primary duties would be. Lori hesitated, watching Jonathan's guarded look.

"Okay." Lori closed the basement door, sealing the chill from the October evening downstairs before turning back to him.

"I'll be working with the missile teams."

Lori breathed in slowly and released it just as slowly. Every assignment meant new terminology, but something in Jonathan's demeanor warned her that she wasn't going to like this. She'd been hoping for a law enforcement assignment, which would keep him on base and close. This sounded more ominous, like it wouldn't be family-friendly. "Missile teams. What does that mean?"

Jonathan tapped the top of Kay's head. "Honey, let go please." As she obeyed, Jonathan put Charlie down on the floor, and the kids ran off to the room they shared. "It's a ten-day rotation: five days in the field, five days home. The first three days home will be regular office hours, then we'll have one day at the commander's discretion and one day off."

Lori struggled to process the information. "What does five days in the field mean? Are you living out there?"

"Yeah. The closest sites are forty-five minutes away, but others are a couple of hours. Some are even farther, but the guys assigned to them hop on a helicopter for the trip out."

"So five days gone, then five days home, and only one or two days of rest in between every eight or nine-day work week."

"Right. I probably won't know if I'm working days or nights in the field until we're headed out, but all the hours on base will be day shift."

"So they expect some of you to shift your sleep every five days?" This didn't sound good. Jonathan was already having problems sleeping since his last deployment out of Alaska to Prince Sultan in Saudi. Actually, if she were completely honest, she'd noticed some problems after the first deployment, but she didn't like to think about it. No sense borrowing trouble, as she'd heard one of the older ladies in her family say. They certainly didn't need more trouble than they already had.

"Maybe. But not necessarily all the time. I could be assigned a lot of day shifts."

Lori caught herself chewing on her lip. Concerns flooded her mind, but what could she do? She was just the lowly wife. A dependent. An inconvenient attachment to the man in uniform. Jonathan's commander would not care about her thoughts unless Jonathan became a risk to himself or others. And she'd learned at Elmendorf that speaking up to anyone he worked with, anyone in his chain of command, only brought trouble down on him.

She took a deep breath. "Okay. When is your first rotation?"

"I go out Tuesday."

Tuesday. Reality slammed into her, and she steeled herself not to visibly react in a negative way. In four days he would be gone from the home more than he was in the home. Lori took a deep breath, doing her best to slowly release it. She could do this, or God wouldn't have moved them here. Right?

TWO

LORI STRETCHED HER NECK and rotated her shoulders to relieve the tightness. Sitting in her new gliding rocking chair by the large windows that covered one full wall in her living room, she looked at the sparsely furnished room. The newly purchased glider was what she'd wanted ever since she'd found out that she was pregnant with Kay. The room also boasted a recliner given to them by Joy on her and Reese's way back West because it wouldn't fit in their new home on Ellsworth. Beyond the recliner and between two chairs sat a small table for holding coffee cups, a desk for the family computer, and a dining table with four chairs. Designed for a full living and dining room set, the room with its limited furniture was left with a lot of open space, and Lori wondered again if she'd made a mistake putting the couches downstairs with the television. Of course, this arrangement would give her a little quiet time to read while the kids played wildly downstairs.

Lori sighed and looked at the book in her lap. She knew reading would get her mind off what her family lacked, but even when she tried to read, her brain wouldn't focus on the words. She alternated between fretting about Jonathan's work schedule and listening for sounds of Joy's arrival. The kids were bathed and ready for bed in their one-piece, footed jammies, currently sitting together on Kay's bed looking at books while waiting for Emily to come through the door, and Jonathan was downstairs relaxing in front of the television. This is what she wanted, right? A quiet sitting area for reading, away from the TV? Or would that merely create more distance between her and her husband? His trouble getting enough sleep at night was affecting other areas of their lives.

Finally, Lori heard a car door shut. She jumped up to look out the kitchen window and saw Joy's dark head ducking inside the side door of the silver minivan. "They're here!" she said, barely loud enough for her own ears to interpret.

Her heart raced like she hadn't seen them in months, even though they'd stopped in South Dakota when they'd traveled back from Ohio two weeks ago. She opened the basement door and yelled over the sound of the television in the basement, "Jonathan! They're here!"

The kids came running. Lori met them at the front door, which was already standing open. She picked up Charlie so he could see through the glass on the screen door. Kay stood on tiptoes, able to peek just over the edge of the aluminum frame where the glass started.

Reese walked up the driveway, his tall, lanky form making Emily look so little in his arms. He whispered in her ear and pointed toward the front door. She turned to see and squirmed to get free. Socks sniffed around the front yard until Emily started running. Her ears pricked up, and then she raced Emily to the door, pulling eight-year-old Zach, who was holding onto the leash, across the yard. Lori laughed, shaking her head at all the time she'd wasted in obedience-training classes with that dog. Socks was never going to heel.

Lori opened the door and let the excitement burst through. Zach released Socks into the house, and she paced between investigating her new surroundings and sniffing each member of her family. Six-year-old Sarah began a monologue of how interminably long the trip lasted, her dark brown hair bouncing along with the recitation. Kay led Emily down the hall to her room, and Charlie vacillated between hugging Socks and checking out what Emily was doing. It was mildly controlled chaos, and Lori relaxed into it. People she loved filled her home. The stress of sleeping problems, work schedules, and pregnancy emotions faded to the background.

"Whew!" said Joy, slumping through the door and leaning against the entry wall. "That is a monotonous drive!" Her arms overflowed with coats and a couple of Walmart plastic bags.

Lori smiled, remembering their trip just a couple of weeks earlier.

"Yes, it is." Jonathan closed the basement door behind him.

Lori took the coats from Joy and put them in a pile by the closet, opening the door to begin hanging them up.

Joy held up the bags. "Where do you want me to put these wet diapers?"

"Kitchen trash right over there is fine." Lori hung up two of the coats before realizing she would need at least one more hanger.

"We couldn't even find a good place to stop to change Emily," said Reese. "I finally just pulled over on the side of the road."

Jonathan nodded. "Yeah, once you leave Rapid City, there's not much along the way except for Billings."

"And that one Wendy's, Dad," Zach called out from his

slouched position in the old recliner without looking up from his hand-held game device.

"Yeah," said Reese, "about forty-five minutes outside of town here."

"Lots of ranch land." Joy went to work on the remaining coats while Lori grabbed two hangers from the bedroom that was slowly becoming the nursery.

Joy haphazardly wrapped a coat around the hanger, adjusting it slightly. "So are the missile sites on the ranches?"

The coat slid off, landing in a pile on the ground. Lori giggled and took the hanger. "Let me do that. This isn't your strong suit." Joy smiled her appreciation.

Jonathan leaned back against the wall separating the kitchen and dining area. "The government leases the land from the ranchers. I've heard a couple of horror stories about trying to run a war exercise and cows getting in the way."

Reese laughed. "Adds some unpredictability to it."

"Can we go see a missile site?" Zach asked.

"You drove by a couple on your way here," said Jonathan. "There's not much to them above ground. It's basically just a chain link fence in the middle of a field."

"Can we go in one?"

Zach looked hopefully at Jonathan. Joy ruffled the hair on top of his head. "Afraid not, son. Those would be classified areas, and last I checked, you don't have clearance."

"I don't have clearance to see any of the cool stuff," Zach muttered.

Reese chuckled. "Come on. You have clearance to see the inside of our van, and it has a lot of unclassified material that needs brought inside."

"I'll help," said Jonathan.

Zach dragged his feet as he trudged behind the men. "Isn't that exciting? Woo-hoo. I get authorized to handle the..." The rest of his monologue got cut off by the screen door slamming shut behind him.

Lori raised her eyebrows, looking at Joy. "Got some attitude going on there?"

Joy rolled her eyes. "Yeah. The last week has been interesting. But I've noticed it gets worse when he's hungry, so do you mind if I make him a sandwich?"

"Of course not. How about snacks all around? I know it's a little late for food, but I don't expect the three little ones will be calming down anytime soon."

THE SUN SHONE BRIGHTLY Saturday morning, and the temperature hovered around forty degrees. Lori and Joy corralled the kids into vehicles, Emily hopping in with Charlie while Kay chose to sit beside Sarah. The men got in the drivers' seats, and Reese followed Jonathan on the short drive off base to the Lewis and Clark Interpretive Center on the banks of the Missouri River. They explored the exhibits, marveling at the life-sized model of men heaving a loaded canoe up the falls, giggling as the kids struggled together to pull a rope that was connected to the same weight as the historical men had pulled on the original expedition in the early 1800s. Even with Lori and Joy adding their muscle, the rope barely budged.

Before heading back to Jonathan and Lori's for lunch, everyone bundled up in coats and walked a short distance on the River's Edge Trail. None of the falls were in sight from the Center, but the short bluffs were beautiful and the water current gentle. Lori couldn't wait to see the area come alive in the spring.

Joy and Lori sat down on a couple of boulders as Reese and

Jonathan helped the kids look for good skipping rocks in a small gravel area at the end of the pathway.

"I can certainly tell why Montana is called Big Sky Country."

Lori followed Joy's line of sight up the Missouri. "Yeah. I can't quite decide why, but the sky just seems to overpower everything. At times it can be this incredible blue, almost like blue Jell-O. And even when it's full of clouds, there's just..." Lori faltered, not having the vocabulary for what her eyes had seen in their short time here. "It's just massive."

The wind blew a lock of Joy's hair into her face, and she swept it back. "I feel very small."

"You don't see this in Rapid City?"

"No, not like this." Joy took a deep breath. "Maybe since it borders on the badlands. Or maybe because you feel more like you're in a city. I don't know exactly. It's just...not like this."

"Yeah, even when we were driving through Kansas and Nebraska, the sky stretched out with the plains for as far as I could see. Or years ago, when we drove through west Texas and everything just stretched before us." Lori shook her head. "It just looks different here. I've never experienced anything quite like this anywhere else we've been."

"It's like a glimpse into how big God is."

"Hmmm," said Lori. "Now there's a thought."

"What? How big God is?"

Lori hesitated. Joy was the closest thing to a best friend she'd had in years, yet she couldn't quite share the fears trapped inside her. Something held her back, wouldn't quite let her be honest with Joy. Lori wasn't sure she was being completely honest with herself. Too many things threatened the delicate hold she had on life. No, Lori wasn't ready to answer Joy's question.

"So how do you like your new squadron?"

Thankfully, Joy went along with the change in topic.

"It's going well so far. I've been assigned to one of the supply warehouses for the B-1s, and I got a couple of young troops assigned to me."

"So you're babysitting while handing out airplane parts all day?"

Joy nodded as she shifted on the rock. "Pretty much. It's not that much different from all the deployment gear I handled at Elmendorf."

"Any chance of deployment for you?"

"Not really. They could always send me to keep track of parts overseas, but they're more likely to let me stay put. We've got several young, single airmen anxious to get into the action in Afghanistan. As long as they keep volunteering, I can stay out of the rotations."

"You're so close to retirement now..." Joy had deployed several times in her eighteen years with the Air Force and found herself in danger more than once. War wasn't the only threat to military members on foreign soils.

"Yeah. I'd go, of course, if they asked me to, but Emily is so young. I'd really like to stay put with Reese and the kids."

Lori watched the five kids as they played with their dads, thinking of all her friend would miss if she deployed. When they'd first arrived at Malmstrom, they had driven past an outdoor air park with a small collection of old airplanes. On prominent display near the front was a Minuteman Missile. Jonathan's job here was to protect missiles just like that one—with his life if necessary. And she was grateful for it. Many friends were heading off to war while others, like Joy, were on an increased operations tempo to support those going. But manpower at nuke bases was kept steady, and the assignment meant Jonathan would be stateside.

As Lori listened to Joy talk, she was thankful for the assignment at a nuke base and the hunks of metal buried deep all over Montana. A five-and-five rotation to the field wasn't so bad, considering the alternatives.

REESE AND JOY RETURNED HOME, and Jonathan started rotating out into the field. He worked days his first rotation, twelve hour shifts from 6:00 a.m. to 6:00 p.m. Lori was hopeful that would be normal, but his second rotation was nights. They only had one car, so posting days meant getting the kids up at 4:15 in the morning to drop Jonathan off at the squadron in time to get his gun and be ready for Guard Mount, the briefing they received before they went out to their assignments. These were the days Lori tried to get the kids to go back to bed when they got home, or at least to take naps after an early lunch.

The days passed quickly, and Lori paid attention to the news that affected so many they knew. NATO's Standing Naval Force in the Mediterranean was working to prevent movement of weapons of mass destruction, and the Northern Alliance fighters had just taken Kabul on November 14. With four more journalists ambushed and killed just a few days after that, many around the world were on high alert and sacrificing their upcoming Thanksgiving holiday for the greater good.

But not the Braxton family. It was business as usual on Malmstrom, and unlike last year, Jonathan would be home for Thanksgiving this year. Lori had sacrificed in other purchases for herself and the kids while Jonathan was out in the field so she could purchase a small turkey and a few potatoes for their holiday dinner in two days. It wasn't much, but it was better than the Christmas when she and the kids sat at home alone and ate cheap, frozen pizza.

Knowing Jonathan would be exhausted from working overnight until six this morning and then staying up to pack his bag and wait for his ride back to the base, Lori made sure their bedroom was neat and ready for him to nap if he wanted to do so. She debated whether or not to put the kids down for a short rest. When Jonathan had called his first night out, he'd said he was at Sierra. All she knew for sure was that meant he was located at one of the closer sites. Depending on when his relief left Guard Mount, he could be home anywhere between noon and 3:00 pm. Which perfectly spanned Charlie's naptime. Kay would be fine as she'd been weaning off naps for several months, but Charlie did not handle interrupted sleep well. No, it was better to deal with a tired Charlie, possibly putting him to bed earlier than usual if necessary, than trying to deal with a short-tempered Charlie because he'd been yanked out of bed before he was ready. Lori opted to let them play.

The clock ticked on. She kept doing little things around the house, dusting the bookshelf and straightening up Kay's room. But when she finished mopping the kitchen and saw the clock read two o'clock, she was frustrated. Charlie could have gotten in a good nap. She looked at Socks lying on the floor in the living room. "How am I supposed to schedule anything if I never know when he's going to call?" The dog huffed at Lori and rolled onto her side.

Charlie walked in holding his cup up. Lori took it from him. "Do you want something to drink?"

He nodded. "Milk?"

She picked him up, and he snuggled against her, his head on her shoulder and his arms tucked between their bodies. She rubbed his back, savoring the rare moment of stillness in her boy.

"Kay, do you want a snack?"

She heard a commotion of toys falling to the ground before

Kay burst out of her room and came running. "Yes!" The child slid the last few feet across the wood floor, throwing her arms around Lori to stop herself.

Lori laughed at her and reached down to push Kay's bangs out of her eyes. "Okay, let's find something to eat."

Charlie lifted his head and repeated his question. "Milk?"

She walked into the kitchen just as the phone rang. Lori sat Charlie down so she could answer it and pour his milk at the same time.

"Hello?"

"Hey," said Jonathan. He sounded exhausted. "We just got back to the base. I still need to turn my gun in, but I should be ready to go in about twenty minutes."

"Okay. We'll be there."

She hung up the phone and looked at the kids. "We've got to pick a snack for the car so we can go get Daddy."

Kay jumped up with her hands raised above her head. "Yay! Daddy!"

Charlie tried to mimic her, jumping up and down a couple times. "Daddy!" But his attention soon returned to his initial request. "Milk?"

Lori screwed the lid on his sippy cup and handed it to him. Bending down to his level, she said, "Yes, milk. And now shoes so we can go get Daddy."

Kay was running for her shoes before Lori straightened, the snack totally forgotten. No matter how irritable Jonathan became due to his little bits of sleep, his baby girl loved him deeply. Lori wondered how long that would continue if Jonathan's sleeping, and thereby his attitude, didn't improve.

THREE

Lori never felt Jonathan come to bed, but when she woke to the touch of Kay's hand on her cheek Thanksgiving morning, he was there beside her. He'd gone to sleep soon after getting home Tuesday, sleeping about five hours before getting up as Lori was putting the kids to bed. They'd sat on the couch together for a while, relaxing and watching TV. She could tell he was exhausted, so she hadn't asked much of him. She simply enjoyed sitting with him, his arm around her.

Jonathan had worked at the squadron on Wednesday as scheduled and came home that afternoon with the news that Thursday was a Family Day. Everyone on base who wasn't critically needed at their job was released to enjoy the holiday at home with their family. Lori dreamed of sleeping in, enjoying a good meal, and some time of everyone together doing something fun. She should have known that sleeping in was a luxury she wasn't going to enjoy with Kay in the house. The child had an internal clock that woke her up early no matter what time she went to sleep the night before.

Loved ones were hundreds of miles away, but Lori longed

for family and cherished memories as she thought of the over-flowing tables of food and crowded dinners she'd enjoyed as a teen. Thanksgiving was the start of her favorite time of year, and she wanted their first Thanksgiving at Malmstrom to be a special day that they would remember for many years. Her table wouldn't compare in volume of food or people to her memories with her aunts and uncles, but she could do something more than she usually did.

Lori sat up, swinging her legs over the side of the bed and pushing her shoulder length locks away from her face. She gave Kay a quick hug before grabbing her hand and quietly leading her out of the room. With the door shut behind them, she crouched down to Kay's level and whispered, "We'll let Daddy sleep some more, okay?"

The child nodded, and they went to the kitchen to find some breakfast.

Looking again at the contents of her cabinet, Lori searched for anything she could do to make the holiday more special. A box buried in the back of a bottom shelf gave her an idea. "Kay, would you like to help me make some brownies for dessert later?"

Kay nodded, as Lori knew she would. Her girl loved to bake. If only she had a mom who liked to work in the kitchen. Lori sighed and tried to push the thought away. This was not the day for nagging regrets. Today, she could put the effort in and make this day special for all of them.

After sliding the brownies into the oven, Lori went to work on the table. She didn't own any tablecloths, but she grabbed a jar candle she'd been using for decoration on a bookshelf and placed it in the center of the table. Its dark red color would add a little fall ambience to their meal, although she wasn't sure she could make herself light it while they ate. Putting her kids that close to live fire didn't sit well. She thought about lighting it while she worked in the kitchen, but quickly dismissed that as the table was on the other side of a wall from where she would be standing. Not having a line of sight wasn't a good thing with little ones, especially Charlie. Instantly, thoughts of the toy area in the basement flooded her mind again, but she pushed them back. She would not feel guilty today. She would be a good momma and a loving wife.

Pulling four sheets of paper from the printer, Lori looked at Kay. "Want to color us some placemats? You can make them bright and happy. We need lots of orange and yellow and green."

"Okay!" Kay's little feet ran to the bookshelf where they stored the crayons, and she quickly returned with lots of colors. "Pink. We need pink too. And purple." She named each color as she sat it down in front of her paper. "And boo. The sky is boo so we hafta have boo too, Momma."

"That sounds delightful, baby girl. Lots of color is exactly what we need today. Can you make one for each of us?"

Sweet Kay was already coloring, her tongue sticking out the left side of her mouth like it always did when she concentrated. "Yep. One for you and one for Daddy and one for Charlie and one for me. I'll do it. I will."

The hours passed, and the house filled with delicious smells. The turkey filled with stuffing was ready to come out of the oven, and the potatoes were peeled, diced, and sitting in a pot of water on the stove waiting to be cooked. Yet in the midst of all the preparations, Lori stood alone. The kids were playing in the basement, and Jonathan slept.

She'd given the kids a snack at their usual lunchtime, knowing that the holiday dinner wouldn't be ready to eat until around 2:00. But now at 1:30, she hesitated, uncertain how to proceed. Should she wake Jonathan? Should she postpone dinner until he got up on his own? She chewed her lip, weighing her options. Finally, knowing she'd have to feed the kids one way or the other, she opted to wake him.

Quietly approaching the bed and bending down beside him, she laid her hand on her husband's shoulder. "Jonathan?"

His response was slightly delayed. "Hmm?"

"The food will be ready in about thirty minutes."

"Okay."

He didn't move or open his eyes. Lori hesitated, not sure what to do. Doubts flooded her mind. She'd been wrong to wake him. She should have let him sleep. She knew how little he got some nights.

Returning to the kitchen to turn on the potatoes, she felt trapped. If he did get up, he'd be expecting dinner in thirty minutes just like she said. But if she didn't finish the preparations, if she waited instead until she heard him up and moving, what would she feed the kids in the meantime? Her dreams for the day slipped away, buried in her uncertainty. *This day isn't special to anyone I live with,* she thought. *I shouldn't have worried about deviled eggs or making sure I had Jonathan's favorite broccoli or some corn for Kay. I could have saved us the expense of a turkey and just served peanut butter and jelly.*

As the tears started to fall, Socks nudged up behind her. Lori bent down and wrapped her arms around the dog's neck, burying her face in the thick, black fur. "My faithful girl," she murmured.

Socks patiently stood there in Lori's hug, allowing Lori to cry out her frustration. As she heard the potatoes starting to bubble, she sat up and rubbed the dog's ears. "Thanks, Socksy."

Kay topped the stairs. "Mom? Can we eat now?"

Lori turned toward the potatoes and wiped her face with the kitchen towel, hoping Kay hadn't noticed anything. She stirred the potatoes, testing their tenderness even though she knew they hadn't boiled long enough. "How about you help me get the table ready with all the food. And then we will eat."

"Okay!" Such enthusiasm. Maybe there was hope for the day.

"You need to wash your hands first. And what's your brother doing?"

"He's coming," she said as she charged down the hall.

"Kay! You're not supposed to leave him on the stairs." Lori crossed the kitchen and looked down the steps, seeing him about halfway up. "Hang on, buddy."

Never content to be left behind, particularly by his sister, Charlie continued climbing as Lori made her way down to him. Scooping him up and depositing him safely onto the kitchen floor, she closed the basement door behind them.

While the potatoes boiled and Charlie climbed into his booster seat at the table, Kay and Lori got the food on the table. Considering what they normally ate, it looked like a feast, the small table overflowing with their efforts. Turkey, stuffing, broccoli, corn, and a few biscuits. She just needed to finish the potatoes and pour the gravy into a bowl.

As Lori finished mixing the potatoes into a creamy mound, Jonathan came into the kitchen. He wrapped his arms around her waist and leaned his head on her shoulder. "Sorry I slept so late."

Lori didn't know how to convey her disappointment, and truthfully, it was more of a conversation than she wanted to have. She refocused her attention on making the day special. "That's okay," she said, turning in his arms to face him. "It's got to be hard flipping between a day and a night schedule."

"Yeah. I didn't sleep all that well in the field either. Not much more than four or five hours per day."

"That's not good. Were you just having trouble adjusting to sleeping during the day?"

He shrugged and stepped away from her to pick up Kay, who had run in the moment she saw him and hugged his leg tightly. "I don't know. Maybe." He walked toward the table. "The turkey smells good."

Lori allowed him to change the conversation, but worry niggled at her heart. His sleep had been disturbed for months, but they'd dismissed it at first because he'd just returned from deployment. And then because they had a lot to do to get ready to move. And then because of the stress of the war and the new job. Surely his body was just adjusting to all the recent changes in their lives, right?

JONATHAN POSTED BACK TO the field on Monday, and Lori faced her first prenatal visit on Tuesday at thirteen weeks pregnant. As she'd sat in their empty base house in Alaska on September 11, waiting to see if the housing inspector was going to make it through the chaos of increased security to their appointment to sign out of base housing, she'd felt a bit nauseous. Later that afternoon, they'd stopped at the commissary, and Lori had grabbed a pregnancy test, not sure she was excited about another baby. The two she had were a lot to handle.

The next morning, armed with a positive test, she and Jonathan had discussed their limited options. They were driving out the next day, facing thousands of miles of wilderness. If they delayed long enough for a doctor appointment, they could be fighting snow through the Rocky Mountain passages. Instead, they chose to purchase over-the-counter multivitamins to sustain her until they checked into their new base.

Now, looking at the small clinic on Malmstrom, Lori wasn't

sure they'd made the best choice. The new hospital on Elmendorf was, well, huge. Lots of doctors and nurses and more clinics than she knew existed, and the Malmstrom Clinic was a little L-shaped building that clearly limited their capabilities. Still, she didn't have another choice, so she lifted Charlie out of his car seat and walked in with Kay and a cartload of doubts beside her. Nervousness about seeing a new doctor aside, she was also anxious about the reception her children would receive. The women's clinic at Elmendorf enforced strict rules about no kids in the exam room. Hopefully the Malmstrom Clinic was more lenient and would accommodate Kay and Charlie, because she didn't yet know anyone. It was take them with her or not be seen.

She checked in and found a seat in the waiting room, occupying the kids with a book until her name was called. An airman showed them into an exam room where Lori pulled out a baggie of crayons so the kids could color on the disposable paper covering the exam table. Thankfully, they only had to wait a few minutes before another airman walked through the door.

"What can we help you with today, Mrs. Braxton?" The woman remained standing, leaning against the closed door of the small room.

Lori recognized the three stripes on her sleeves denoting her rank as Senior Airman, but she could never remember the difference in the insignias on the chest. Was this a medic or a nurse? "I'm several weeks pregnant." Lori felt her face heat slightly from admitting something so personal to someone she didn't know.

"Okay. Have you seen a doctor yet?"

"No. We just recently moved from Alaska."

Kay pushed Charlie's hand away from what she was coloring. "No, Charlie. You color over there."

The airman began writing in the folder she carried. "Did you give birth to both of these children?"

"Yes."

Charlie put his crayon down and started to explore. Lori absent-mindedly laid him on his belly across the doctor's stool and gently spun him around.

"Okay, so you know the general process. We'll put in an order for your prenatal vitamins. You can pick those up down the hall at the pharmacy. Try to get some light exercise every day, which I'm guessing won't be hard with these two." She smiled, watching Charlie spin. "Eat healthy, aim for lots of fruits and veggies, drink milk, no smoking—all those kinds of things." She made several check marks on her paper before looking back at Lori.

"Okay."

"We are not equipped for prenatal care here at the clinic, so we'll get a referral in for you to see one of the obstetricians in town. And I'll go put in an order for your initial labs so that will be done by the time you have your first appointment. We'll forward that on to the doctor you choose."

"Okay. How do I do that? Choose a doctor?"

The medic reached behind her for one of the papers stuck in an organizer hanging on the wall. "Here is the list of the OBs in Great Falls that accept military insurance. Look that over while I get your vitamins ordered, and I'll be back to record your choice. We'll let TriCare know, so you shouldn't need to do anything."

She stepped out, and Lori looked over the list of seven doctors while Charlie tried to spin himself. The obstetricians appeared to all be at one of three different clinics around town, which simplified the decision somewhat. Not knowing any of the names, Lori thought through her previous experiences. The doctor for Kay had been a male, and they'd been in transition during Charlie's pregnancy so she'd seen a variety of males and females. The females had been a little more compassionate, though, which Lori appreciated. If she went with a gender qualification, that narrowed her choices to three doctors: Vicky, Georgia, and Susan. With nothing else to go on, she made her choice based on the name she liked best.

The medic came back in the room. "Have you made a decision? Or do you want to call me later with the doctor of your choice?"

Lori knew that postponing the decision wasn't going to make this easier, and it wasn't like she knew anyone to ask or was going to drive around and ask to meet each one. "I'll go with Vicky Donnelly."

The airman made notes on her folder. "Excellent! We hear lots of great things about her."

Lori felt a little better about her choice, even if it was based on something somewhat vain.

"Okay. I'll get the referral in for Dr. Donnelly. In the meantime, go out our doors to your left and down the hall to the lab. I've already put in the order for blood work, so they should be ready for you soon. If you have any non-pregnancy related problems, we'll see you back here."

"Okay. Thank you."

Kay reached over and pulled on the airman's camouflaged uniform shirt. "'Scuse me, please." She pointed over to the exam table. "May, ummm, please may I take my picture home, please?"

"Absolutely. Let me tear that off for you."

"And Charlie's too?"

The airman smiled, ripping the paper above all the artwork and carefully rolling it up before handing it to Kay. "And Charlie's too."

Lori breathed a sigh of relief. She still hadn't met her

doctor, but at least she could switch to the prescribed prenatals, saving them the money they'd spent on the over-the-counter multivitamins. She was also, finally, under a doctor's care.

She grabbed Charlie's hand and led her children down the hall as directed, nibbling on her bottom lip. Did she make the right choice for a doctor? They all had to be somewhat competent to pass the medical exam and get licensed, right? And the airman did say that they heard lots of good things about Dr. Donnelly.

Doubts niggled at her, filling her thoughts and circling around until she was a mess of confusion and uncertainty. Would she ever be able to make a decision and not wonder if she'd made a poor choice?

FOUR

DECEMBER 2001

JONATHAN CRUMPLED THE report in his hand. He knew the list by heart because it screamed at him during the night: significant credit card debt, house that won't sell, new baby on the way, little kids at home. The Life Skills Support Center counselor sympathized with the weight on his shoulders.

"Truthfully, if all of this wasn't weighing on you, I'd be more concerned," he had said.

"Well, that's reassuring," Jonathan had told him, "but what am I supposed to do in the meantime? The doctor is worried about my insomnia, and honestly, I'd just like to know without a doubt that I'll be able to sleep when I get the chance to."

Their financial situation worried him more than he'd admitted to the counselor because what base leadership already knew was throwing up caution flags on his file. He'd received his line number to sew on Staff Sergeant, but that, and the corresponding pay raise, wouldn't come until spring. So he hadn't complained when the counselor had picked up the phone in front of him and made him an appointment with a financial counselor at Family Services. However, his hopes had been dashed again. This guy seemed knowledgeable and competent, but he wasn't much help.

"Look, debt consolidation is rarely the way to go because of how most of them go about the process. But it wouldn't help you anyway. Your wife has done an excellent job keeping the interest rates on your credit cards low. I doubt if any of them could offer you anything better than what you've already got."

Lori had written down their expenses for Jonathan prior to this appointment. The numbers stressed him out so much that he barely looked at their check register or bank account. He let her handle all of it, not wanting to think about where their money went every month. He just knew they didn't have any extra to spend.

"She has the grocery bill well under control—heck, it's even lower than I would have suggested before I looked deeper at your numbers. You have the loan on your car, but it's not outrageous, and the small bike loan, but it's not out of line for a second vehicle option for you."

Jonathan was frustrated. How could they be doing everything right and he still feel like they were drowning? "So, what do we do? Where can we cut?"

The counselor shook his head. "The only possibility I see is your check to the church—but even that's not going to be enough."

Jonathan sat back in his chair, hesitating for only the briefest moment. "No. We're Bible-believing Christians, sir. I respect that you may not agree with me, but our tithe is not up for debate."

Tossing his pen down on the file, the counselor also sat back in his chair. "Look, I'm okay with that. I don't go to church, but

I can appreciate how much your faith means to you. Regardless, the bottom line is that it doesn't really matter. We're not looking for better discipline or a couple hundred dollars to pinch out of some budget category where you are overspending. We're looking for a mortgage payment to cover that house in Ohio, and it's just not here—even without the car loans and the tithe."

"So what do we do? We can't keep doing what we've been doing." Jonathan stood. He needed to move, but the room was so small that pacing was almost useless. He took two steps to the wall and turned back toward the counselor. "We've put the house on the market before and got nowhere, and we can't underprice it because we don't have any equity in it. But we're going further in the hole every month with the rent being under the mortgage amount and the added cost of the property manager."

He took three steps to other side of the room and spun on his heel. "I don't feel like I can buy my kids a Christmas present or a birthday cake. I can't even..." Jonathan paused, thinking about Lori. He knew she didn't really want much from him other than his time and attention, but he wanted to grab hold of the world and give it to her. He wanted to buy her a fancy anniversary ring for her finger and all the books she dreamed about reading. He wanted a house of their own that she could decorate however she wanted, and piles of presents for each kid on every birthday. He took in a slow, deep breath and blew it out before walking back to his chair and sitting down again. He had no words to convey all his fears. It was too personal to share with this stranger he'd probably never see again.

"I almost never recommend this," the counselor said quietly, "but I truly don't see another way."

Jonathan looked the man in the eye, waiting for the news

that he clearly didn't want to say. Jonathan wasn't sure he wanted to hear it.

"I recommend you file for bankruptcy."

LORI LOOKED AT HER TWO kids sitting at the breakfast table. It was December 4, still early in what was usually her favorite season of the year, yet she had no desire to think about Christmas. Thankfully, great grandparents and an aunt had sent money to buy gifts for the kids, and the other grandparents would send enough presents that neither Kay nor Charlie would realize that nothing under the tree was actually from their parents. She'd scraped enough money together to mail small things to their parents, but what was she going to do for Jonathan?

The conversation from the night before still echoed in her heart and mind. *Bankruptcy.* She couldn't fathom it and hadn't reacted well to Jonathan's report of his conversation with the financial counselor. They'd signed their names on the loan paperwork and credit card agreements, promising to pay. They'd given their word. What did it say about them if they backed out now, even if it was through legal means?

Guilt overwhelmed her—a heaviness for not knowing how they could pay all they owed but also shame for even considering asking for a way out. No, she'd been right to insist they ignore the counselor's advice. Right?

Lori shook her head, trying to clear her thoughts. Jonathan would be hesitant to bring it up again, especially so soon after her angry outburst yesterday. Today was supposed to be one of Jonathan's two days off before he returned to the field on Thursday. He was sleeping in with her blessing, partly because she didn't want to face another conversation about their finances and partly because he needed to catch up on his sleep. Lori planned to occupy the kids until he woke up by letting them help her set out some of their Christmas decorations, but then she hoped they could do something fun together as a family. She didn't know exactly what that would be, and she didn't really care as long as they could put last night behind them. At least for today.

Jonathan got up about ten o'clock and spent time playing with the kids. Just as they were beginning to discuss lunch ideas, the phone rang. Her husband sounded official on the short conversation. After hanging up, he sighed deeply as he crossed to sit back in the recliner with Kay. "Mandatory Commander's Call. I have to report at 2 pm."

Lori was irritated. She saw all her plans go flying out the window again. She sat in her glider, trying not to take her frustration out on him. "What could the commander possibly want to talk to everyone about?"

Jonathan shrugged. "Could be almost anything. Could be something happened in the field that they don't want anyone else doing. Could be an update on the war situation and how it affects us. Could be about the spring inspection that we have to pass. It shouldn't take too long. I've been told that they are normally only about thirty to forty-five minutes or so."

Lori sat quietly fuming but determined not to show it. This was neither Jonathan's choice nor fault, she reasoned to herself.

Jonathan reached across the chair to grab her hand. "We'll take the kids to the park when I get home."

Kay's gray eyes lit up, and she looked at her daddy. "The park!?" She looked at Charlie, who was building with his wood blocks in the middle of the floor. "Charlie, do you want to go to the park?"

"Yes!" He dropped the block he was holding and started to

get up, but Kay sat up in Daddy's lap and put her hand out like a policeman stopping traffic.

"We get to go later, Charlie. Daddy has to leave. We'll go when Daddy gets home again."

Charlie nodded, clearly accepting this change to their plans far better than Lori was. "Okay. Park later," he said as he sat back down with his blocks.

Lori pulled herself out of her self-pity and made sandwiches for everyone. Jonathan put on his uniform, and they all waved goodbye before settling in to put lights and garland on the artificial Christmas tree they'd inherited from her grandfather. Every once in a while, Lori would check the clock, irritation growing as time ticked by.

Three o'clock. Surely he'll be home any moment. Three thirty. What could the commander possibly want to say that takes this long? Four o'clock. Could she have missed some news? Lori took the kids downstairs to play and turned on the television to see if something big was happening around the world. More than once, the news channels reported battles and skirmishes before the units were able to notify the families at home. But nothing seemed out of the ordinary. Or, at least, out of the new war-torn ordinary.

At five o'clock, she looked uncertainly at the kids. She'd given them a snack at three thirty, anticipating Jonathan being home any moment to go to the park. But she and the kids would all be ready for dinner soon, and she didn't have any idea if she should cook for Jonathan or not.

Choosing to keep it simple, Lori prepared a box macaroni and cheese to add to their usual peanut butter sandwiches, calling the kids to the table. She tried hard not to watch the clock as she ate and cleaned up the kitchen, but by seven o'clock, worry was winning. Unfortunately, she could do nothing but wait. If something had happened to Jonathan,

Security Forces or someone from the squadron would knock on her front door. That hadn't happened. She certainly wasn't willing to call any of the wives that she had yet to meet on the squadron roster. She'd likely sound like a fool wondering if their husband was home or if they had any news. No, she would just have to wait.

She thought about taking the kids downstairs to watch a movie to help pass the time, but she didn't want to miss a knock on the front door. Sounds didn't always travel well down the stairs. Instead, she tried to distract herself and the kids by helping Kay put together a puzzle and Charlie build with his blocks in the middle of the living room floor within sight of the front door.

Finally, just after 7:30, Jonathan walked through the door.

"Daddy!" Kay jumped up and ran to wrap herself around his leg as was her usual habit. Charlie followed and claimed Jonathan's other leg.

Clearly exhausted, he put his hands on the tops of their heads. "Hey, guys. Let Daddy go, okay?"

Kay released him, and Lori grabbed Charlie and positioned him on her hip. "I was getting worried."

Jonathan just shook his head. "We showed up to helicopters waiting for us to load up for a recall exercise."

"Recall? Like war games? Like where you practice retaking a missile facility from control of the bad guys?" That would explain the long afternoon.

"Yes." Jonathan walked into the kitchen and filled a glass with water. "They flew us way out to one of the Tango sites. From there, it shouldn't have taken as long as it did, but apparently the rancher didn't get enough notice to have his cows out of the landing zone. So the helos had to drop us at an alternate landing site over a mile away, and we had to hoof it to the site."

"Didn't they tell him you guys were coming?"

"I overheard someone say that they only gave him an hour's warning. So when we flew over, I saw him out there, but he still had plenty of cattle to move." Jonathan opened the fridge. "Are there any leftovers from dinner?"

"I'll make you a sandwich." She put Charlie down and grabbed the bread off the counter. Pulling the peanut butter from the pantry, she said, "So, you were dropped off a mile out?"

"Yeah. I got assigned to carry the big M60, which adds significant weight to my gear. And none of us were prepared for this. They didn't tell anyone that this was happening. Thankfully, I had my winter gear in my A-bag in the trunk and was able to grab it and put it on. But a couple of the guys were out there in just their uniforms and gloves."

She shook her head. The weather had been slightly warmer than usual, but the temperature outside today probably hadn't exceeded 45 degrees. "Bet they'll be putting their coats in with their gear tonight."

"After the Shirt releases them. He was not happy some of the guys didn't have all their gear."

"That's not a conversation I'd want to be part of."

"Me either."

"Daddy," Kay said, patiently standing beside him. "Can we go to the park now?"

Leave it to Kay to remember the promised outing.

"Not tonight, sweetheart," he said. "We'll try again tomorrow. Maybe while Mommy goes to see the doctor."

———

LORI'S DOCTOR'S APPOINTMENT the next day seemed to go well. She'd gained about fifteen pounds already, weight gain being normal for her family. Her mother had gained so much weight with Lori's older brother that the doctor had put her in the hospital on a restricted diet. With Kay, Lori had gained thirteen pounds in the first trimester, so she wasn't concerned about the extra pounds with this third baby.

"Everything is looking good so far," said Dr. Donnelly. "The baby's heart rate is in the 140s, right where it should be. Your weight gain is a little higher than I'd like, but it doesn't sound unreasonable considering your history. When we do an ultrasound, do you want to know the gender?"

"Yes, please." Lori liked to plan, and simple things like whether she should be thinking blue or pink helped tremendously. Not to mention she and Jonathan were having great difficulty coming up with a name. They needed all the help they could get, even if it was merely to narrow the possibilities down to either a boy or a girl.

"All right." She made a notation in Lori's chart. "What about amniocentesis? You might remember that's a test to check for chromosomal abnormalities and some fetal infections. It can—"

"No." Lori interrupted the doctor. "We don't care about abnormalities."

"I understand. But even if the test comes back reporting issues and you plan to keep the baby, the test can help you prepare—"

"No, ma'am." Lori shook her head. "I appreciate your concern, but the answer is still no. We'll love our baby regardless, and we'll deal with whatever comes when it gets here. Quite honestly, I have enough going on right now, and I don't need one more thing to worry about."

"It could put some of those worries to rest."

"Yes. Or it could exacerbate them." Lori stood firm with the decision she'd made with each of her pregnancies. God was in control, and she would trust Him with the health of this baby.

It was one of the few things in her life she was actually pretty good at releasing to Him.

"All right then." Dr. Donnelly made another notation on Lori's chart and then tucked the pen behind her ear. "Keep trying to do some light exercise every day, eat healthy, and make sure you are drinking lots of milk. I'll see you next month."

Lori walked to the front desk to check out, her mind whirling with the doctor's words. Did she make the right decision? Jonathan wouldn't care one way or the other. He trusted her to make these choices. Maybe she should have done more research before being so firm with the doctor. Could she change her mind? Should she?

Lori handed her chart to the woman sitting at the desk.

"Did everything go well?"

Lori answered automatically, trying to set her mind at ease. "Yes."

A smile seemed to come easy for the perky brunette. "That's good. Now, let's see. Dr. Donnelly wants to see you back in four weeks, so how about Thursday, January third?"

She looked at Lori expectantly, and Lori hesitated. She was sure they were used to clients with packed calendars, but Lori didn't have that problem. Friends or activities outside of Sunday morning services were nonexistent. "Ummm, that's fine."

"Is two o'clock okay? Or I have four-thirty available."

"Two is fine." Lori hoped it was fine. She wasn't sure what she would do if Jonathan was in the field or couldn't take time off work. How hard was it to reschedule an appointment here? She should probably ask, but Lori didn't want to be a bother. She made a mental note to count his workdays out ahead of time so she'd be ready for this when she was back in January.

The woman clicked a few keys on her keyboard before

looking at Lori again. "Do you have other children?" She stood to grab a business card from the counter and leaned forward to write the date and time of the appointment on it. A small, gold cross dangling from her neck caught Lori's eye.

"Yes. Two."

She smiled. "Any time you want to bring them to your appointments, they are welcome, especially for these early ones where we're just checking vitals and such. A lot of big brothers and sisters like to hear the baby's heart beat."

"Okay." Lori knew Kay would enjoy that, and it eased her concerns about Jonathan's availability.

"Now, before you go, we also need to schedule your ultrasound. Do you know when you would like to do that? You'll be twenty weeks about January eleventh, so any date around there is good."

She looked at the little calendar they had posted on the counter and tried to process Jonathan's schedule, but her brain wouldn't work as fast as she wanted it to. "I'm not sure when my husband will be off. He works an odd schedule."

"Military?"

Lori nodded.

"No problem. A lot of our patients are, so we understand." She pointed to the card Lori still held in her hand. "Just check his schedule and call us back at that number. Anyone who answers the phone should be able to help you schedule that. The doc would just like it done between your next two appointments, which will likely be four weeks apart. Let's see..."

She looked at her computer screen again. "That would put your following appointment about January thirty-first. So if you could come in for the ultrasound between the fourth and twenty-fifth, that would be perfect. Just try to give us at least two or three weeks' notice so we can fit you in the schedule without too much difficulty."

Lori nodded. "Okay."

"Other than that, you're good to go. If you have any problems or questions, give us a call. Otherwise, we'll see you after the New Year. Merry Christmas!"

"Merry Christmas." Lori walked away feeling a little overwhelmed. The woman was more than friendly. She was cheery, genuinely happy. Lori wondered if she was always like that or if Christmas brought it out in her. And where could Lori find some?

KANDAHAR, THE POWER BASE for the Taliban, had fallen. Backed by the American and American-allied militaries, an anti-Taliban fighting force under the command of Sherzai and the Eastern Alliance under the command of newly-appointed-President Karzai pressured the Taliban into surrendering the city. The Taliban had lost control of their last major city in Afghanistan. Americans celebrated, hoping for the best.

Osama Bin Laden was still in locations unknown, and the Bonn Agreement was being finalized in Germany on how a postwar Afghan government might look. But rotations, alerts, and recall exercises continued as scheduled on Malmstrom, completely unaffected by the possibilities brewing in the rest of the military world. Jonathan rotated out on Thursday, working another rotation of night shifts.

Sunday morning, Lori got the kids breakfast and then ready for church. They'd found a small Baptist church just a few blocks outside the main gate. The congregation was small but friendly, and, except for the Sundays Lori was pressured to take her turn in the nursery, she got a short rest from the kids and a boost to her sagging spirit.

The church was built like a split-level house with the bottom floor half-buried underground. This meant Lori had to climb about ten steps to get through the front doors and an additional eight to get to the second floor where Charlie's class was located. She always tried to arrive early to give Charlie plenty of time to get his determined self up those stairs on his own.

She walked slowly behind him as he climbed the steps, dropping him off to a sweet, older lady who was already singing *Jesus Loves Me* to the little ones in her care. Lori didn't yet know her name, but her presence was comforting. She felt like sitting in a corner of the room with her and soaking in whatever it was that she had. That might be a better alternative than going to the adult class and pretending like she had it all together.

Kay bounded down the stairs toward her classroom while Lori followed behind as quickly as she could. She just didn't have the gumption this morning she needed to keep up with her active children. The break from them during Sunday school would be a welcome relief.

"Morning, Lori!"

She looked up to see Patty Kendall's tall, skinny frame paused on the stairs below her. Patty's son Micah charged up the stairs to zoom around Lori at the last minute. Micah was just a couple of months older than Charlie, but his frame was as solid as Charlie's was slight. Both strong-willed children, they were opposites in almost every other way.

"Hi."

"Jonathan's in the field?"

"Kay, hang on!" Her daughter brushed her bangs out of her eyes as she looked back at Lori, but she stopped right where she was. Lori was thankful for Kay's easy obedience. "Yes," she said, looking at Patty. "He'll be home tomorrow afternoon."

Patty nodded. "Good. I never like it when Dillon has to go out on alerts, but I'm so thankful he's just gone 24 hours. I don't know how I'd survive five-days like you do all the time!"

Lori smiled, trying to come up with something nice to say. The difference in field requirements for officers and enlisted were stark. In addition to the much shorter time frames, Patty's husband only went out about twice a month, only taking him out of the home for about four days out of every thirty. She wasn't sure how she was supposed to respond to Patty, though. She didn't like going five days at a time without her husband. She didn't like counting days on a calendar to see if he'd be able to participate in the next holiday or if they'd have to celebrate on a different day. She didn't like parenting alone, or going through pregnancy alone, or not having a back-up available if she didn't feel good. She didn't like missile duty! But she couldn't say all of that out loud. It would be...ungrateful. Disparaging of her husband's career.

Truthfully, she might end up in a puddled mess right here on the stairs if she started letting herself be openly honest about this duty station and her life. And she could never do that.

Additionally, she remembered their friends currently serving in Afghanistan. The spouses at home didn't know where their loved ones were or what dangerous mission they were being asked to do next. They didn't know how close that last bomb hit, how much shrapnel was possibly imbedded in their skin while they were still healthy enough to assist in one more attack, or where the enemy would strike next. Guilt flooded her heart as she thought about Army friends whose husbands left right after 9/11 and had only had one or two phone calls in the ninety days since. They had no idea when their loved one would be home, and their only assurance that their soldiers were still alive was the fact that no one in uniform had shown up on their doorstep. Yet. How dare she think about complaining about five-days!

And so, Lori found the determination to smile at Patty. "At least I know he'll be home every week."

Patty smiled, taking a couple of steps forward and reaching out to place her hand on Lori's arm. "That's right. You've done deployments."

I nodded. "Two. About a hundred days each."

"I guess I'm spoiled. Dillon's career ties him to just three or four bases, and they're all stateside. I don't have to worry about all that."

Kay started making a game of jumping up and down the stairs, and Lori wanted to get her off them before she fell. The last thing she needed right now was a four-year-old in a cast. Lori grabbed her little hand as she jumped up two steps to land beside her. "I'm going to take Kay down to her room. I'll see you in class?"

"Save me a seat."

Yes, Lori would gladly save Patty a seat. She liked her, even though she didn't feel like she could relate to her. Would she ever find a friend here that she thought might understand all she was going through?

FIVE

LORI'S STOMACH CHURNED as she looked at the envelope the mailman had left in their box. The return address was from the law firm they'd hired to help them file for bankruptcy. She still couldn't believe she'd signed that representation agreement. But attorney Ashley Hodges had been utterly calming to the turmoil in Lori's soul.

Jonathan had set up the appointment and asked Lori to go with him, "just to listen," he'd said. He'd argued that they couldn't make a wise decision if they didn't have more facts. Lori had agreed to both appease him and end the conversation. She was too exhausted to think through what he was saying, and she really didn't want to fight with him again. She just wanted all of this to be done and over with—the finances, the sleeping problems, the constant emotional strain.

Just a few days before Christmas, they'd walked into a small reception area on the third floor of a five-story building in downtown Great Falls, an apparent skyscraper by the city's standards. Ashley had swept into the room with a flurry of instructions for the lady at the front desk, then greeted them professionally and led them back to her office that wasn't much bigger than the desk and three chairs it held. But what most caught Lori's attention was that Ashley sat behind that desk and acted as if she had all the time in the world for Lori and Jonathan. She'd relaxed, answered their questions, given them things to think about, and offered advice that seemed reasonable.

The plaque with Joshua 1:9 sitting on the filing cabinet near the desk had helped too. *Be strong and courageous. Do not be afraid; do not be discouraged, for the Lord your God will be with you wherever you go.* She loved that the verse was from Joshua, the name of the street that they currently lived on, and Lori could definitely use a bit more strength and courage right now. But would the Lord really be with them if they walked willingly into bankruptcy? She wasn't so sure.

Not one to let things remain unsaid, when Ashley saw Lori's eyes linger on the verse, she'd asked if they read the Bible. Jonathan had responded that they did, but Lori suspected they didn't read it quite like Ashley did. Ashley talked about God like He was a companion, a guide, a daddy. Like she *knew* Him. She emanated grace and peace, but Lori kept running up against the wall of shame and fear for the reason they were considering hiring her in the first place.

"How do you do it?" Lori glanced at Ashley but quickly looked away again. She couldn't believe she'd said that out loud.

"Do what?"

Now Lori had to trudge ahead or come up with some explanation for her bold question. She fought for as much courage as she could muster. "Reconcile helping people file bankruptcy with the Bible? Aren't we breaking our word? Didn't we promise to pay? Didn't God tell us to let our yes be yes?" Lori couldn't pull her eyes away from Ashley's gaze now. She didn't really know what she expected the woman to say, but she'd just attacked Ashley's chosen career while laying all her doubts on the table.

The attorney took a deep breath before responding. "Those are good questions, and to be honest, I'm not sure I can give you the answers you are looking for."

Lori felt tears forming that she didn't know if she could hold back.

"I can tell you that Old Testament law allowed for two things. Well, more than two things, but two that are important for our discussion here: A Sabbath Year and a Year of Jubilee. After six years of hard work, they were to take a Sabbath Year of rest. Farmers were not to sow the fields or prune the vineyards. The land—and therefore the men who tended it—was to have a year of rest, although they were allowed to reap what grew naturally."

Ashley fingered her cup like this was the most casual of conversations, but Lori hung on her every word seeking the hope, the assurance, that what they were considering was acceptable to God.

"After seven of these Sabbath years, the Jews were to celebrate the Year of Jubilee. During this time, they not only were to refrain from planting the fields, but they were to return everything they held that belonged to someone else. Anything you had sold to another—even if you were forced into selling because you needed the money to survive—that property could be redeemed. And it included more than property but also people who had sold themselves or their children as slaves. Everyone was to go free."

Ashley leaned forward slightly in her chair, clasping her

hands in the center of her desk. "I know this may very well be the most painful moment of your life." She looked directly at Lori. "I'm so sorry that life has brought you to this place."

She paused before continuing, and a tear released down Lori's cheek.

"The Bible teaches that we are to help those who need it, and I believe you need it. My expertise and training is in dealing with the court system and with debtors to provide you some desperately needed breathing room so you can restore your hope, get back on your feet, and provide help to the family beside you that also desperately needs someone to reach out to them with whatever gifts and talents God has provided."

Now, as Lori held the envelope in her hand, Ashley's words came flooding back. Lori clung to them like a lifeline. Could God really use her to help others? What could He possibly have put into her that would make even a minor difference in any other person's life?

JONATHAN SCANNED THE LETTER Lori had left sitting on the dining table. The information needed was overwhelming, including values of their wedding rings based on pawnshop standards. As he'd never sold anything at a pawnshop before, how could he possibly know what one would offer them for their wedding rings? He skimmed farther down the list, noting many of the items wouldn't be too hard to provide. A copy of his most recent pay stub, the name of the tenant in their house in Ohio, copies of old W-2 forms. At least, he assumed this would all be easy to provide. Lori seemed organized, so surely she had all that information somewhere.

He heard her putting away dishes in the kitchen, so he stepped into the doorway. "This is a long list."

She sighed deeply when she saw the letter in his hand. "The attorney's list? Yeah, it is."

"Do you need my help on any of it?" Jonathan wasn't sure why he asked. Lately the commander had been keeping them busy every day they were not in the field preparing for the spring inspection, so he certainly didn't have much time to offer.

"I could use your help for the one that talks about getting written valuations for the vehicles. She wants a car dealership to write down for us what they would give us for the truck, bike, and trailer."

Jonathan swallowed his frustration. What his wife asked for was reasonable, as she didn't know anything about riding the motorcycle and had never driven with the trailer hooked up. Still, it wasn't like he wanted to go do these jobs himself. Of course, he had agreed with the financial counselor that this was the best course of action, then been unrelenting on Lori until she'd acquiesced to talking to a lawyer. It was unfair of him to expect her to do everything.

"Are we going to be able to make another payment to her soon?"

Jonathan hated asking the question, but knowing they'd stopped paying on the credit cards should mean they could pay on the lawyer's bill. The attorney wouldn't file with the bankruptcy court until she was paid in full, so the sooner they paid her, the sooner they could file and the sooner this financial pressure would go away.

His ears picked up on another deep sigh from Lori, one she appeared to try to conceal from him. Maybe he didn't understand how much this was affecting her too. All the more reason to make this happen as quickly as possible.

"I think we can set aside $200 from the mid-January

paycheck, and I hope to have another $100 set aside from the February 1 paycheck."

"So we'll be able to pay her off by the middle of March?"

Lori shook her head. "I don't know. Maybe."

Jonathan wanted to push harder, get more specific answers, but the look in her eyes held him back. The slump of her shoulders and the dark shadows under her eyes told him she was tired, but he felt like he was missing something. The dog lay at the top of the basement stairs watching them, and he could hear the kids playing downstairs. They sounded happy and content.

Then it hit him. The baby! The kids had gone to a friend's house this morning so Lori could go to the doctor without them. He sat the letter on the counter in front of him. "Did you have the ultrasound today?"

"Yes."

"How did it go?"

She shrugged as she turned to the dishwasher and started putting the dishes away again. "They won't tell me anything. I'll find out details when I see Dr. Donnelly at the end of the month."

"But no news is good news, right?"

Jonathan watched Lori, her back to him. Her shoulders moved slightly as she took a deep breath and slowly released it. She half turned toward him, looking him directly in the eye. "No. Sometimes no news is simply that. No news."

What was that supposed to mean? Jonathan felt the sting of an insult he didn't understand. It probably had something to do with him not being available to help around the house or him not coming to bed with her at night. She had no idea how hard it was to want to go sleep but be unable to. His mind wouldn't turn off, and his body wouldn't relax. Neither was his fault. He couldn't even keep from moving his legs; it felt like bugs crawled all over them the moment he lay down in bed.

He spun on his heel and stormed down the basement stairs. If she wanted to be in a mood, he'd let her be in one all by herself. He didn't have to participate. Instead, he'd forget his problems in whatever movie he could find on television. Or, at least, he hoped the television would drown out his thoughts for a while.

KAY'S INTERNAL ALARM CLOCK went off about an hour before the sun's on Tuesday morning, and Lori trudged to the kitchen to help her get a bowl of cereal for breakfast. Walking into the living room, everything seemed brighter than normal. She turned to look out the windows that she still hadn't purchased curtains for and froze.

Snow! It must have started after they all went to sleep because she knew it hadn't been there when she'd put the kids to bed. She'd sat in the living room for a few minutes to make sure Charlie was going to stay in his room, but then she'd gone to bed too. Now, she saw enough snow to cover the grass and make the world look pretty.

She knew Kay would be excited once she saw it, but it made Lori want to bury herself back in bed. Base regulations said she had to shovel driveways and sidewalks within twenty-four hours, and Jonathan had just posted to the field yesterday. He couldn't rescue her. She didn't look forward to the chore, but as the kids would need to be outside with her while she worked, at least they would get in their snow playtime.

Kay came running out of the kitchen, impatient for Lori to follow her. "Come on, Momma!" She grabbed Lori's hand and pulled.

Lori bent down to her level and pointed out the windows. "Look."

Kay turned her attention to the wall of windows. Her gasp told Lori she'd have to find something exciting to occupy her daughter until the sun rose and her brother awoke; otherwise, Charlie would wake to a sister squealing about snowmen, snow angels, and piles of snow coated in syrup.

Several hours later, Lori paused in her shoveling. She knew that when they were finally able to purchase a second vehicle, having only a one-car driveway would mean either parking on the other side of the street where it was allowed, or constantly switching vehicles between the one in the garage and the one in the driveway. But for now, as she leaned on the shovel with her back to the wind trying to catch her breath, she was thankful for only having one small section to maintain.

The snow was wet, which meant that even though it was only about three inches deep, it was heavy. Kay and Charlie were sitting in the yard in their brightly colored snow pants, each with a small volcano of snow before them. Kay had poured syrup into each one, and they were cheerfully eating with plastic spoons. Their little cheeks and lips were rosy, and they were waiting on Lori to help them build a snowman, but they were content for the moment.

Lori looked at the sidewalk that lay before her and the path the kids had carved walking to the elementary school behind their house. The packed snow under their footprints would make the shoveling harder, but Lori didn't have it within her to force all those footprints up. She just couldn't give them a cleanly swept or freshly salted walk, and if the powers-that-be on Malmstrom wanted more, they would have to provide it.

Or kick them out of housing. The thought swirled unbidden in Lori's head, and she sighed deeply, knowing she didn't have the mental capacity for an off-base move, much less the financial ability to pay for the move or the increased expenses of an apartment in town. She returned to shoveling, trying to give more than her aching back and tired arms seemed capable of doing.

She worked diligently, and after what seemed like hours, she turned over the last shovelful of snow. She leaned against the handle of the shovel, cautiously standing more upright, stretching her back against the tightness. Twenty-one weeks had never seemed so very pregnant before.

Kay had been watching closely as Lori worked. Every few minutes she could hear her little voice: "Momma's getting closer to done, Charlie. Soon we can build a snowman." Now, before Lori was ready to yield her back to the bending that a snowman would require, she saw her precious child jump in the air. "Are you done? Are you done?"

The last thing Lori wanted to do was build a snowman. She wanted to go inside and get warm. She wanted to crawl into bed and take a nap. But she chastened herself and reminded herself what a good mother would do: Build a snowman and play in the snow with her children.

Lori held out the shovel toward Kay. "Go put this away in the garage, and we'll build a *small* snowman." It was something. A compromise between what she wanted and what her kids expected. Truthfully, she wondered how small she could get away with.

"Okay!" Her daughter raced toward her and grabbed the shovel, turning to run into the garage.

"Yay! We build snowman this big!" Charlie stood up on his toes and raised his hands above his head.

Lori laughed. "Buddy, we don't have that much snow. But we can make a little one." Thirty minutes earlier, Lori had wanted to curse the three inches covering the ground. Now she was more thankful than she could express that it was only three inches.

"Like my size?" He patted his rounded belly.

Lori shook her head. "No. Smaller. We don't have that much snow either."

Running back to her brother, Kay saved the day. Sort of. "We can each build a snowman, Charlie. Both of us! We will each have our own snowman! But they will have to be smaller because we have to share the snow together."

While this excited Charlie, the thought of helping two children build two creations was more than Lori wanted to think about. And she certainly didn't have snow pants that fit her so she could crawl around the yard like they were doing. When this was done, she'd be a sopping wet mess. She corrected herself. She'd be a sopping wet mess with two happy kids.

She breathed as deeply as the cold wind would allow, hoping for a burst of energy. Her kids deserved better than the whiny mom they had at the moment. Looking at what covered the yard, each snowman would only be about twelve inches high, but she would help her kids and be a good mother. She would be the mother these children deserved in this moment, but would she ever find delight in it?

SIX

FEBRUARY 2002

LORI HAD NEVER FELT SO ALONE. Jonathan had been home, according to the squadron, for four days, yet he might as well have been out in the field. He tossed and turned so much when he went to bed that neither he nor Lori could sleep. After an hour or two, he'd finally give up trying and go to the basement to watch TV, leaving Lori to lie there alone. He'd come back at some ridiculous time of the morning, finally able to drift off to sleep, only to get up with his alarm and go off to work.

Today was his day off before posting back out to the field tomorrow, but his habit for the last month had been to sleep through the day in an attempt to catch up on the sleep he'd missed for the nights prior. Lori wanted to spend the day together as a family, but her expectation had been that he would miss out once again, not doing anything with them. She'd been right.

That evening, they sat downstairs watching a movie. It

wasn't what Lori wanted, but at least Charlie was curled up on Jonathan's lap and they were together. Lori looked across the couch at her husband, hoping for a moment of love or attention from him. Instead, she saw a man struggling to stay awake and pay attention.

She quietly asked, "Do you want me to get you some over-the-counter sleep aid?"

He looked at her, eyebrows raised. Shaking his head, he said, "I'm not allowed to take it."

"But it's over-the-counter." She combed her fingers through Kay's hair absent-mindedly. "You've got to get some sleep." Surely the government could see the wisdom in their troops getting adequate sleep.

"It doesn't matter. If they think I'm taking too much Tylenol, they can temporarily decertify me to work with the nukes."

Lori swallowed the grumbling she wanted to express, straining to keep her temper under control. "So sleep-working is acceptable but taking something to get a good night's rest isn't?"

"Sleeping on the job is a big no-no. Even if I sleepwalk while in the field, that could cause issues. Thankfully I haven't done that in months. Right?"

This time, Lori didn't contain her frustration. She didn't care about the sleepwalking, which he'd only done a couple of times in their five-and-a-half year marriage. What she wanted to do was help her husband, but she felt trapped, unable to do anything at all for him. She understood, even agreed with, the principles behind the stringent requirements of the Personnel Reliability Program for all airmen working with the nuclear missiles. But living them out was much tougher. Wasn't an airman not getting enough sleep more of a danger to the program than one who was taking an over-the-counter medicine to help him sleep on a regular basis? Sure, they said removal from the program wasn't punitive, but it sure felt like punishment, even to Lori who wasn't directly affected by all the regulations.

"Lori, we've been over this. A military doctor has to report all medications, and I have to report anything a civilian doctor orders. All of it could put my deployment status under review."

"But you need sleep," she whispered. "And I need you."

He reached over and took her hand. "I know. Let's just give it a little more time and see what happens."

TEARS THREATENED TO FALL as Lori walked back into the house. They'd received another letter from their lawyer. Of course, she supposed she should be pleased. It did indicate the woman was working hard on their behalf. But she'd only turned in her answers regarding the questions from the last letter four days ago. This woman worked faster than Lori was prepared to deal with.

Walking over to the dining table, she sat the other mail down and ripped open the lawyer's envelope. Two more full pages of questions greeted her. Confirmation of the motorcycle trailer's value, suggested changes to their new monthly budget, questions about the house in Ohio, and more covered the pages. It was too much. She really was going to cry, and she never cried. Well, almost never. The tears seemed to come easier these days.

"Anything good?"

She hadn't heard Jonathan come up behind her. It was the day before he posted out to the field again, and again he'd slept until mid-afternoon. "No." She wasn't in the mood to offer long explanations.

He placed a hand on her back. "You okay?"

All manner of unkind thoughts exploded in her head. She spun around to confront him. "Okay? Seriously? You want to know if I'm okay?"

He held his hands up in surrender, backing up two steps. "Forget I asked."

"But that's just it! I don't want to forget you asked. Because it's the most you've cared in days."

"What's that supposed to mean?"

She saw his temper flare, but she didn't care at the moment. Maybe she would in an hour. Maybe later tonight. But right now, she wanted... She didn't know. But she did know that she didn't want this.

"It means that you sleep—all the time. Except when you're supposed to sleep, of course. Then you just sit up and watch TV." Sarcasm covered her tone. A piece of her knew she should take a breath and calm down, but she pushed forward. "You don't interact with the kids on a regular basis, you don't want anything to do with me."

"I can't help when I sleep!"

"You help it all the time in the field! You show up to work on time every day when you're out there. You even get out of bed and do what you're supposed to do when you're here on base. At least, you get out of bed for your commander. But you won't get out of bed for us!"

"If I didn't report to duty, I'd get in trouble, maybe arrested. That has long-term consequences!"

"And this doesn't? You think we're going to be able to continue long into the future like this?" Lori was completely fed up. Her head was certain her husband loved her and their kids, but her heart didn't feel like he did. She felt like the Air Force got more loyalty and respect than she did.

"I have to sleep sometime! I'm sorry that it's only when it's inconvenient to you." His sarcasm countered her own.

"That's not fair! You act like I don't want you to get any sleep."

"Well? That's how it seems. What exactly do you want me to do?"

"What do I want? I want you to go to the doctor. I want you to be honest with them and with me about what's going on. Where your head is. You think I don't know that this is hard on you? But you don't talk to me, and you won't talk to anyone else!"

"I can't talk to them! If they think something is wrong, I could lose my job."

"And what if you don't? Huh? What if you don't talk to them? How long do you think you'll be able to hold on to this illusion that everything is fine?"

She could see the defiance in his eyes. Jonathan was angrier than she'd ever seen him before. He held her stare for several seconds before turning his gaze out the back windows. He shook his head to some internal argument he wouldn't let her be part of. He was sealing himself off from her again.

"I've had enough."

He stormed back to their bedroom, and Lori called after him. "What is that supposed to mean?"

He didn't respond, and she certainly wasn't chasing after him. He was the one who had stormed off. He could be the one to come back and start the apologies. But when he returned, he was fully dressed in jeans, a long sleeved shirt, and hiking boots. Without saying a word, he barged out the front door, went into the garage, started his motorcycle, and sped down the road.

Lori stood at the front screen door watching him leave. She

didn't know what his leaving meant, what his final words meant. The impact of what she'd said and thought returned to her. Running to their bedroom, she closed the door so hopefully the kids wouldn't see her. Bursting into tears, she sat on the edge of their bed. What had she done? How could she have lost control like that?

"God," she said through her sobs, "I can't do this anymore. I don't want to live like this. I'm not even sure," she paused, rubbing her belly and thinking of the baby boy within. "I'm not even sure I want to live," she whispered. "But you gave me this child to love and protect, so I can't harm myself. But I don't know what to do, Lord. I don't know what to do."

She allowed her tears to flow for as long as they came. Slowly, she calmed and found herself listening for sounds of her children coming upstairs or her husband coming in the front door. She had to pull herself together, but she also knew that she didn't want to be who she was. "How do I change this, Lord? Where do I start? I meant it when I said I didn't want to live like this anymore, but I feel like I can't fix any of it. It's too much. It's too big. What do I do?"

The silence of the house closed in around her. She walked to the little half bath connected to their bedroom, running some warm water over a washcloth to wipe her face. She looked at herself in the mirror and asked again, "What do I do?" She waited in the silence, hoping for an answer.

It was then that the whisper came. "Start within yourself."

SEVEN

MARCH 2002

"WHEN DID THIS START?" The emergency room doctor pulled his stethoscope from around his neck and started listening to Charlie's lungs. Her boy looked so pale against the stark white sheet.

Lori shifted Kay in her lap and tried to think through the fog in her mind. Jonathan had returned home late in the evening after their fight, and they'd found an amiable peace without actually discussing what they were going to do. But the difficulties seemed to keep coming without either of them finding a resolution. She'd asked God to help her, but another hospital visit with Charlie wasn't the answer she was hoping for. "He woke up this morning with what seemed to be a cold."

"Runny nose?"

She nodded. "He was pretty congested, and his nose was crusted over. It started running as soon as I washed his face and has continued all day."

"This same yellowish color?"

Lori nodded again.

"Did you notice a cough?" The doctor felt around Charlie's throat, and Charlie just lay there, not seeming to care what the doctor did to him.

"Not until this afternoon. His throat seemed to be bothering him when he woke up, but I thought it might just be because he'd been breathing through his mouth. So I got him something to drink."

"Did that help?"

"I'm not sure. But if it did, it got worse throughout the day."

"Why do you say that?"

"He played a little this morning, but not nearly like normal. And as the day has gone on, he's been lying around more. He didn't eat much at lunch and completely refused a snack this afternoon and dinner tonight. And over the last couple of hours, he started refusing to drink anything, and he cries whenever he does cough."

"Okay. His throat feels okay although it is a bit red, and he definitely has some wheezing going on in his lungs. So I'm going to order a breathing treatment. We'll let that go to work, and then see how he's doing after that."

Lori nodded, already suspecting that they were heading this direction when the triage medic had commented on his oxygen levels being low. Her poor boy seemed destined for medical problems. Only two weeks ago, they'd been in the doctor's office for an itchy rash on his legs and arms. Eczema, the doctor said. Thankfully the steroid cream was making it better, and Charlie didn't mind giving up some of his baths, which the doctor had said could make the dry skin worse.

But now they were in the emergency room again for a breathing treatment. And, of course, Jonathan was out in the field and couldn't be here to help. He didn't even know yet that anything was wrong. Was this their future? Would she forever be the one burdened with making medical decisions outside of her knowledge? Why would God entrust this child to her when she clearly didn't understand all she was up against with respiratory problems and skin rashes? Would Jonathan blame her for not taking good enough care of his children? What if the doctors reported her to Family Advocacy for the sheer number of medical appointments and emergency care required?

Lori took a deep breath. She knew she had to reign in her thoughts. After her emotional breakdown two weeks ago when Jonathan had stormed out of the house, she had committed to reading her Bible and finding resources to help her understand it all more. A search on the Internet had introduced her to author Kay Arthur, and the downloadable devotional she'd found was opening her eyes to how destructive her own thoughts were to her well-being and marriage.

"I will take every thought captive," she whispered, quoting the verse in Second Corinthians that yesterday's devotion had focused on. Forcing her negative thoughts to quiet, she watched the medic add medicine to a small container and affix it to the oxygen mask. Charlie lay motionless as the airman adjusted the straps that held the mask firmly over his nose and mouth.

"I'll be back in a few minutes to see how he's doing," he said.

Lori thanked him as he walked out and then shifted Kay to sit in the chair by herself while Lori walked over to her boy. She grabbed his hand, looking at his small fingers in her palm. "Every thought captive," she whispered again.

Looking at Charlie, she brushed his hair away from his face. "You're going to be okay, buddy. We all are. You just need a dose or two of the medicine, and then they'll send us home."

THE PHONE RANG. Lori set the book she'd been reading down on the table beside her glider. "Hello?"

"Hey!"

Joy. Hearing her friend's voice, Lori smiled. They chatted frequently over the computer, particularly since Lori had been honest with her about how depressed she'd been in February. But a phone call was rare because of Joy's duty hours and the fact that they were both surrounded by little ones.

"I've been thinking about you," Joy said. "How's Charlie doing?"

Lori sighed. "Much better. Completely back to his usual self. We finished the last of the amoxicillin yesterday, thankfully, so we're off all meds, and the cold seems to have cleared."

"That's good. If you guys are up to it, we were thinking about invading."

"Really? When?" Excitement pulsed through Lori, and she knew Kay and Charlie would be just as excited. She'd have to keep this from them until it was closer to Emily's arrival, or they would drive her crazy asking about it.

"The kids have the week after Easter as their spring break, and Easter is a four-day weekend for me."

Lori spun around to look at the calendar on the wall. She'd been purposely marking off Jonathan's rotations so she could try to schedule things to include him. "Easter. When is that? The last Sunday of the month?"

"Yep, March thirty-first this year."

"Okay, so Jonathan will be in the field until Saturday the thirtieth, but then he'll be home until the following Friday morning. When he's home, he usually gets Sundays off, and if it's a four-day weekend for you, he might get Monday too!"

"Do you think he'll mind if he comes home to all of us there? If we arrive on Friday night? I could try to take a couple days off work, but the tempo has been so increased with stuff shipping out that I'm not sure they'll let me have it."

"I don't think he'll mind, but I'll ask. He should be calling tonight after he gets off shift. I can message you later."

"He's working day shift this cycle?"

"Yes! Thankfully. He has a doctor's appointment when he gets home this time too, to find out the results of the sleep study they did last week." Jonathan still wasn't great about telling Lori all that he was thinking and dealing with, but at least he was beginning to tell his doctor what was going on. It was a start, and she rejoiced in it.

"Does he have any idea how it went?"

"Not really, other than the technician kinda shook his head at him the next morning. We're guessing it wasn't good."

"Didn't Kay have an appointment too? Something with her eyes?"

"Yes, earlier this morning, actually, and that went well. The doctor called it pseudo-something or other. I can't remember the medical term, but he said her eyes aren't really crossing or lazy. It's just that the bridge of her nose hasn't formed yet, and the way her skin there lays around her eyes makes it look like they sometimes cross. He wants to check her one more time in six months to be sure, but he's fairly sure that we don't have anything to worry about." Between Jonathan and Charlie's health issues and her pregnancy, Kay's concern seemed tiny. But now that the weight of it was gone, Lori acknowledged it had been heavier than she'd realized.

"That's great news! You needed some of that."

"Yes, we did. But I think I needed God more."

"What do you mean?"

"Well, the more I read that book I told you about—the Kay Arthur one—the less I think about all the problems going on in my life. I don't know exactly why. I'm still exhausted all the time, but I'm almost thirty weeks pregnant and have two young kids that I'm largely raising alone while Jonathan lives in the field. I should be tired."

"Most definitely."

"I also started trying to talk to that lady at church more, Patty. Kay really likes her daughter, and she has a son about Charlie's age too. I think our families would get along well. It's hard—you know how difficult it is for me to make friends. But, I'm trying."

"You are happier than I've heard you in a long time. I can't remember when you've sounded more positive. It's been a while, probably before we all left Alaska."

"Yeah. I can't really explain it because my life isn't any different than it was three or four months ago, but I guess it's just God making changes inside of me. The outside stuff is still hard, and I still have to remind myself every day that God is in control. But I don't have to fight to believe it every second I'm awake any more."

"I can't wait to see you."

"Me too," said Lori. "Me too."

JONATHAN STORMED out of the commander's office and headed to the parking lot. The weekend with Reese and Joy had the best he'd had in a while, and he and Lori seemed to be doing better ever since he'd admitted to his doctor that his sleep was worsening. But things at work were not improving. He'd held his tongue for the last twenty minutes like a good troop should, but now all he wanted to do was pummel something thoroughly.

"What is this horse—"

Jonathan couldn't believe the amount of cussing that had streamed from the man's mouth as he'd thrown the reports from Jonathan's doctors down on his desk. It wasn't that curse words were uncommon to his career field or to military members in general. But typically, mid- and upper-level officers kept a better control on their mouths, especially in official meetings. Perhaps that newly pinned silver oak leaf hadn't soaked into his commander's behavior yet.

The bottom line was that Jonathan was between the proverbial rock and a hard place. On one side, his doctor's diagnosis included severe obstructive sleep apnea and insomnia, along with restless leg syndrome and a small host of other concerns. On the other side, his commander didn't believe the reports. To save his marriage, he needed to do what he could to heed the doctor's advice. To save his career, he needed to ignore all of it and continue with the status quo.

Except he knew that the status quo wasn't going to work either. Jonathan was exhausted and sleeping only a few hours every other night. His body couldn't keep going like it was, and eventually he would make a mistake on the job that would cost him his career anyway. Maybe more.

Unlocking the car door, Jonathan slid behind the wheel. He sat there, staring at the building that housed the irritating man in charge of his future, considering his options. His thoughts turned to Lori. Last night he'd walked upstairs to find her sitting in the middle of their living room floor laughing as she and Kay played a board game. The woman could no longer get up off the floor without help, but she'd willingly sat down to spend a few minutes doing what Kay wanted to do. She was a good mother, and she deserved a good husband. A husband who was more available to her than the sleepwalking zombie she currently had.

The decision had to be that simple, even if it meant more anger-filled meetings like he'd just endured. His wife—his family—was worth it. Starting his car, he headed to the clinic to make an appointment with his doctor. Surely, the man could do something to help.

EIGHT

THE COMMANDER SHARED a last name with the bad guy from one of Lori's favorite movies, which she found quite appropriate. The man was a menace, or at least he was for Jonathan. Still disputing the doctor reports, he refused to make most of the allowances the doctor wanted to try—things like keeping Jonathan on day shift for a month. He had kept him at the squadron for one rotation, allowing a ten-day trial of a prescription sleep aid, which had worked amazingly well. But, it was on the list of medicines not allowed under the Personnel Reliability Program. Jonathan couldn't take it and work around nuclear weapons.

The sleep clinic had recommended a continuous positive airway pressure machine, commonly known as a CPAP, to combat his sleep apnea. Although he appreciated the better quality sleep he got when he actually slept while wearing the mask, trying to get to sleep while connected to a hose that was forcing air up his nose was a major adjustment. Sometimes it was worth the fight. Sometimes it made his insomnia worse, and he gave up.

Regardless, the commander was convinced that Jonathan merely wanted out of field duty. The man insisted that her husband was going to the doctor, submitting to sleep studies, and acting like a general guinea pig for the medical community's latest idea simply because he didn't want to post to the field. It didn't make any sense to her.

Jonathan had shared a little about the tirades his commander went on whenever Jonathan had to report the latest medical reports to him. The most recent tantrum—because Lori couldn't think of a better word for it—included the man yanking Jonathan's worldwide qualifications and ability to carry a gun. Jonathan was a cop on a base that was filled with cops whose primary mission was security, and yet he couldn't carry a gun. What exactly was he supposed to do? Keep order and oversee maintenance at one of the dorms for unaccompanied airmen, apparently.

Lori tried not to fret as she thought about her husband's current meeting with the man. She didn't even like calling him commander because that carried a level of respect that she didn't possess. It was probably for the best that she wasn't invited to the meeting.

Still, questions buzzed in her head. Since Jonathan couldn't work around nuclear weapons, would they be receiving orders to a new base? Were they required to wait a specified period of time to see if things improved? If not, how quickly would they push them out to the next assignment? After all, she was thirty-six weeks pregnant, and she remembered well how difficult the journey to Alaska had been when she was at thirty-eight weeks with Charlie, not to mention the move into a new apartment about a week after he was born.

"I will take every thought captive," she said to herself as she cleaned up the kitchen after lunch. She'd been learning to turn her concerns into prayers, so she took a deep breath. "Okay, God, I'm really not sure what to ask for. If I'm honest, I don't like Montana."

She paused from wiping the counter and looked out the small window facing the front of her house. "Well, that's not exactly true. Montana is okay. But Malmstrom—"

She stopped again and thought of Patty, who had just invited them over yesterday for the kids to play for a couple of hours. She'd enjoyed that immensely, and both Kay and Charlie had played hard enough with Patty's kids that they had come home exhausted. A couple of other ladies at church were quickly becoming friends too. "No, it's not even Malmstrom. It's Jonathan's commander. And Jonathan's health."

She finished wiping the counter and went to the top of the stairs to listen for a moment. Kay was chattering as usual, directing her and Charlie's play. Lori imagined Charlie was half-listening, half doing his own thing, also as usual, which brought forth a smile. They were so different.

She sighed and walked to the living room, looking out the wall of windows past the elementary school to the open wheat fields and big sky beyond. "I want Jonathan to be healthy and happy, but I guess I don't know what that means or what it will take for that to happen. Lord, if we need to move, then move us. If Jonathan needs to change careers, then plant the idea in his head and help him know what to do to make that happen. You are in control—I know that. Help me to have a peace about it no matter what that blasted man..."

Lori paused again, grimacing at her words. "I probably shouldn't have said it quite like that, Lord, but you know who I mean. Just give Jonathan wisdom and me peace. Please. And if you could provide a healthy dose of that sooner rather than later, I'd appreciate it."

LORI AND JONATHAN WALKED hand-in-hand through the hospital doors, his touch steadying her nerves for what was coming. On Tuesday, Dr. Donnelly had shared some concerns about the baby's position. At thirty-eight weeks, he should be head down and ready to go, but instead he had his head buried in her ribs. Like Charlie, their new little boy liked to sit diagonally in her torso. Lori was so short that she frequently had to lean to one side or the other to give him more room. If she forgot, he'd squirm and kick until she shifted positions. Lori wasn't sure whether this boy was that big or that long, but either way, she was anxious for him to be out on his own.

The doctor wanted to see Lori Friday morning at the hospital to do an ultrasound. If he had turned and was ready to go, they'd be patient and try to let the delivery progress naturally. But if he hadn't turned, she wanted to do an immediate C-section to prevent any potential problems.

Lori wasn't sure what to think. She'd had Kay naturally and Charlie by cesarean, so she knew what to expect in both situations. She was ready to be done with the emotional turmoil pregnancy had presented her with this time and eager to finally hold her baby. She was thrilled that they'd finally agreed on a name for him: Austin. But whether she was admitted for surgery or sent home to wait, today would be difficult for her.

Jonathan's immediate supervisor at the dorms had told him to go to the appointment with Lori and report in. If she was having the baby today, then Jonathan's request for ten days of leave would be approved starting immediately. If she was sent home, they'd hold the leave request until she went into labor.

Lori was thankful that at least one person in charge on the base was easy to work with.

Lori saw Dr. Donnelly when they stepped off the elevator in Labor and Delivery, standing at the nurse's station, making notations in a chart. She greeted them, and they waited patiently while she finished.

"Let's go to this room over here." She motioned to her right. "I believe the nurse has everything ready for us."

Inside the room, Lori saw the familiar ultrasound machine set up near the bed.

"Just go ahead and lie down. We'll check the position of the baby before we do anything else."

Jonathan walked to the other side of the bed beside Lori, and a nurse walked in as Lori lay back on the stiff surface. Dr. Donnelly pulled the machine closer and grabbed the bottle of ultrasound gel. Lori pulled up her shirt, and Dr. Donnelly squeezed a generous amount of the cool gel on her stomach.

"All right now," the doctor said, moving the transducer probe around to see the child within. "There's his spine..." She moved the probe, following the spine down Lori's stomach. "That is not a head."

The nurse behind her confirmed it. "Nope, sure isn't."

"Just for grins and giggles," Dr. Donnelly said, "let's go up and look." She moved the probe up toward Lori's right ribcage. "Yep. There's his head." She took a quick measurement before quitting. She grabbed a couple of paper towels from the tray and wiped the gel off the probe before returning it to its hook on the machine. Then she faced Lori. "So, he hasn't turned around, which, as we discussed earlier this week, can cause some problems if you go into labor."

She wiped most of the gel off of Lori, then handed her a couple of paper towels to get the rest herself. The nurse rolled the ultrasound machine out of the way and quietly waited for Dr. Donnelly to finish.

"The current size of his head also gives me some concern about cephalopelvic disproportion, which you've already mentioned with your other son."

"What is that?" asked Jonathan. Lori was glad he spoke up because she couldn't remember talking with the doctor about disproportionate anything.

"That's when the baby's head is too big to fit through the pelvis."

"Ah, yes," said Lori. "Charlie was diagonal with his head in my hip, but when they tried to push him into position and break my water, he flipped on them. Once they delivered him, the doctor said that even if we'd tried to go naturally, a cesarean probably would have been required anyway because of his size."

"Exactly. I think we're facing the same thing here. With your permission, I'd rather circumvent the problems we already suspect as well as everything else that could happen and just get you prepped now for a C-section."

"So we're having this baby today?" Lori reached for Jonathan's hand.

Dr. Donnelly nodded at the nurse, who then left the room. "As soon as you sign all the paperwork the nurse is going to bring to you. They'll get you prepped for surgery, and I'll go check the operating rooms. As soon as you're ready and one is available, we'll get this going."

Lori squeezed Jonathan's hand. Her first thought was of the alarm she'd felt when Charlie was born. "Last time, I didn't handle the spinal anesthesia well."

"What do you mean?"

"I know that I won't be able to move my legs, and I knew it then. But, as soon as they delivered Charlie, I panicked. I couldn't talk myself through it, and the anesthesiologist had to give me something to knock me out."

"Got it. I still want to try the spinal because it's better for you if you can talk to us throughout the procedure, but we'll be ready to intervene if necessary."

Lori took a deep breath and felt Jonathan envelop her hand in both of his. "Okay. Whatever you think is best."

AUSTIN'S BIRTH HAD GONE smoothly, except for the small panic attack that had started the moment Lori knew the baby was safely out. The anesthesiologist had been ready and had inserted a needle of medicine into Lori's IV drip the moment she'd alerted him that the panic was building.

Now, Lori sat in the glider in her living room, contentedly rocking Austin as he slept. Kay quietly read in her room while Charlie napped, and Jonathan was back to work at the dorms. It was monotonous for him and not significantly different from corralling their three children, he said, but at least he was now home every evening. Although she tried to protect him from having to get up too often in the night with the baby, she appreciated the help he offered. Parenting three kids was a big adjustment.

She'd come home from the hospital to several letters regarding their bankruptcy. The date for their hearing was set for June eleventh. Jonathan's schedule with the dorms was easy enough that he'd be able to go without any problem, convenient for the squadron as they'd have to produce him even if he was still posting to the field. They'd also received paperwork from an Ohio Clerk of Courts that the bank that held their mortgage had filed a motion for a default judgment. Lori didn't fully understand that, but she knew she wasn't expected to do anything, so she just filed it.

The latest information from Jonathan's sleeping issues was not encouraging. One report said his REM sleep included moderately severe obstructive hypopnea and apnea, and his periodic leg movement index was more than thirty episodes per hour. She wasn't sure what was normal for a sleeping person, but that sounded like a lot to her.

The doctors wanted Jonathan to improve his sleep hygiene, of course. But that was not going well. He tried, and the CPAP helped when he could get to sleep, but adjusting to the air hose presented problems. He tossed and turned so much that he frequently woke up with the hose twisted around him. Once it was snugly wrapped around his neck!

"Lord," Lori prayed as she held Austin's small hand, "give the doctors great wisdom as they try to help Jonathan sleep. Do what you will with his career, and help me retain the peace of this moment no matter what the days ahead look like."

Lori hesitated as she thought through her words. What did she just ask for in her quest to trust God more?

NINE

SEPTEMBER 2002

THE SANCTITY OF TRUTH WAS not as black and white as people wanted it to be. In Lori's college ethics classes, she remembered classmates who had argued that something was either true or it was not. A logical argument for sure, but in situational ethics, true didn't always mean right. Reading the Bible was changing her thinking, softening her heart, and cementing truth in her mind. She had a lot to learn.

Rolling over on the air mattress to see the time on the portable clock, she decided eight o'clock was late enough. They had driven to South Dakota the day before to visit Reese and Joy for the weekend, and all of them had stayed up too late just sitting and catching up. She'd been awake for a while. Not wanting to wake anyone up, Austin in particular, she'd lain resting on her makeshift bed. Now, though, she was ready to chance it. Quietly walking up the basement stairs of the tri-level base house, she heard someone moving around in the kitchen.

"Good morning," she said, rounding the corner and seeing Joy standing at the coffee maker.

"Hmmm" was the grumbled response.

Lori chuckled as she went to the fridge to find some juice.

"I'm hoping the kids all sleep for at least another hour." Joy interrupted the flow of coffee to pour herself a cupful.

"Or at least Kay lets them sleep another hour."

Joy smiled back at her. "Yeah. That. I definitely don't have any early risers."

Joy and Lori sat at the small kitchen table, enjoying the peace for as long as their six kids would allow them.

"How did Austin sleep?"

Lori stretched her legs out on the chair across from her. "He was up about five this morning, just long enough to eat a bit. He should be awake again any time. How have you been feeling?" She motioned to Joy's ever-expanding waistline.

"Pretty good. This baby is really taking it out of me though. I come home from work utterly exhausted."

"Well, it's not like it's your first baby, and neither of us is twenty any more."

"Hey!"

Lori smiled at her friend. "You got what? Three months to go?"

Joy nodded. "Yep. An early December baby." She played with her cup for a moment, and Lori felt like her friend was looking for the right words.

"What?"

Joy looked at her. "I don't know. You seem more...settled somehow."

"Settled?"

"I know that's not the right word, but I'm not sure what to call it. You're more relaxed, more at peace."

"Hmmm. That's probably because I am." Lori took a drink of her juice.

"Are you finally okay with the bankruptcy? Are things with Jonathan's commander settling down?"

"Yes, and no. The commander is still being a jerk. In fact, he seems to be blatantly trying to kick Jonathan out of the service. Right before we left, Jonathan wrote a letter to the medical board that convened after his apnea diagnosis. He's asking to be reinstated, or at least reassigned. He has a meeting coming up about all of that in a couple of weeks. We're not sure how they're going to rule."

"From what Jonathan was saying last night, it doesn't sound like the man was ready to be in charge."

"No." Lori shook her head. "He definitely needs more leadership training if he's going to be successful."

"So what is it then? What's changed with you?"

"Well, you know I've been more intentional about reading my Bible."

"Yeah, that study you sent me on prayer is really good. I'm not done with it yet, but I'm working through it."

"Good. I'm glad you're enjoying it." Lori ran her fingers through her hair, pulling it away from her face. "I was reading in Exodus a couple weeks ago, and something caught my attention. Remember the story of Moses's birth?"

"Yeah," said Joy, standing up to get more coffee. "His mother hid him for a while and then put him in a basket where the Pharaoh's daughter would find him."

"Right. That was necessary because the Pharaoh was afraid the Israelites would become too numerous and leave. So he ordered the midwives to kill the baby boys when they were born. Do you have a Bible close?"

"I think I left mine in the living room. Let me see."

Joy returned with her Bible, and Lori flipped to Exodus chapter one. "Look, right here it says in verse seventeen that the midwives 'feared God and did not do what the king of Egypt had told them to do.' The king figured it out and called them on it, and they lied to his face. Outright lied."

"Okay." The look on Joy's face indicated to Lori that she was completely lost.

"Here's the thing. They lied, but in verses twenty and twenty-one it says that 'God was kind to the midwives' and 'he gave them families of their own.'" Lori closed the Bible and sat back in her chair. "Look, I still don't completely understand it. When our lawyer explained about the Year of Jubilee and how all the debtors were released, that helped. But then I'd hear the occasional remark that would send me back into shame and guilt—like that one lady I told you about who said to me that Christians were supposed to let their yes be yes and that we had agreed to pay the debt."

"Right, I remember that. She was in a position of authority too, right?"

"Exactly. So her words really hit my heart, and I wasn't sure what to do with it all again. But then I read this, how God honored two women who lied. It showed me that life isn't black and white. Not that I'm advocating situational ethics or relative truth, because I'm not going that far. I still believe in an absolute right and wrong, but I think we forget that God's right is sometimes different than our right. Does that make any sense?"

"Sure. It reminds me of that verse in Isaiah where God says, 'For My thoughts are not your thoughts, neither are your ways My ways.'"

"Precisely." Lori walked to the sink and rinsed her glass, setting it off to the side to use again with the breakfast she and Joy would be cooking for their families soon. She turned and faced Joy, who was sitting at the table watching her. "I don't know that I could explain this concretely to anyone, especially not to someone who's not faced what we were looking at. But I believe God orchestrated the meetings with the financial counselor and with our lawyer. I believe Jonathan was right to lead our family in this direction. It still wasn't fun, and I wouldn't blindly advocate bankruptcy for anyone else, but I see God's hand, and that's good enough." She shrugged. "It has to be, or I'm going to drive myself crazy going in circles about it."

A door opened, and Lori could hear little feet making their way down the creaky, wooden stairs.

Joy smiled. "Do you think it's one of yours or one of mine?"

Lori winked at her. "I'd put money on Kay."

JONATHAN WALKED in the room two minutes before his two o'clock appointment with Captain McLeod, his medical board's consultant for the Personnel Readiness Program, who was already sitting at the rectangular table. The captain stood and offered his hand, which Jonathan shook before choosing a chair around the backside of the table facing from the door. He wanted to be able to see if anyone else entered the room or hovered near the door.

"We're just going to wait a couple more minutes. I spoke with your primary care manager, Dr. Jacobs, and his scheduler was supposed to put this on his calendar for today."

"Sounds good, sir."

"The family doing well? Baby sleeping through the night?"

"Yes, sir, the family is well. Austin is a sleeper. Much better than his brother was, which my wife appreciates."

Jonathan wasn't much for chitchat, particularly with men who could sway those who would decide whether or not he could continue his career in the Air Force. He liked Captain McLeod well enough, but he wasn't entirely convinced he could trust him. Thankfully, Dr. Jacobs entered the room.

"Sorry if I'm late. My last appointment ran long." He pulled out the chair across from Jonathan and sat down.

"No, you're fine," said Captain McLeod. "Well, let's get started. I see from your records, Sergeant, that you were on Clonazepam for a month starting toward the end of July."

"Yes, he was," said Dr. Jacobs. "It's a tranquilizer used to help those with the movement disorder akathisia, which makes it an excellent candidate for treating restless leg syndrome."

"And how did that go?"

"Well," said Jonathan. "I was sleeping eight to nine hours at a time while I was taking it."

"But that was also while you were working all day shifts."

"Yes."

"What side effects did you experience?"

Jonathan leaned forward, placing his arms on the table. "The only thing I noticed was that I started feeling tired around dinner time. I felt more alert during the rest of the day than I have in years." Jonathan tried to relax. More alert was a relative term since he'd been having trouble sleeping for two years. He couldn't remember the last time he'd regularly gotten that much sleep, and he would like to go back to it if the med board would allow it. But he wasn't going to qualify his statement unless the captain asked for more information.

"What other side effects are common to the medication?"

Dr. Jacobs spoke up. "In short-term users, some experience agitation and poor coordination. In long-term users, about a third of the patients experience suicidal thoughts, so they must be watched closely."

Captain McLeod looked at Dr. Jacobs. "That's not encouraging."

"No," the doctor agreed. "Which is why I typically don't recommend it for more than thirty days."

"Doctor, we hand this man a loaded weapon and expect him to be able to use it accurately when necessary."

"I understand that," said Dr. Jacobs, not backing down from the challenge in the captain's tone. "That's precisely why it's listed on the medications not permitted for PRP certification. And I'm not recommending Sergeant Braxton remain on the medicine long term. I wanted him to go on it for thirty days in the hopes that we could get his body re-synced with a healthy sleep pattern."

The captain turned to Jonathan. "And has that happened?"

"It's better, sir. I'm not sleeping quite as well as I was when I was taking the medicine, but I am sleeping better than I was before it."

Captain McLeod tossed his pen down. Leaning back in his chair, he crossed his arms over his chest. "Well, we have a problem, gentlemen. I think the med board would agree to reinstate Sergeant Braxton if his commander would agree to keep him on day shift to allow his body the pattern it needs to sleep."

The captain paused, blowing out his breath before continuing. "I spoke with the colonel yesterday, and he's unwilling to do so."

Jonathan clenched his jaw so he wouldn't say anything that would disparage his character. He could imagine what had been said to the day shift suggestion.

"If the sergeant starts flipping his schedule between days and nights again, I fear we'll be right back where we started. Quickly."

"I expressed the same sentiment, doctor," said Captain McLeod. "The colonel is willing to allow the CPAP machine in the field but will make no other allowances."

"He's forcing me to choose surgery." Jonathan had argued

against it when Dr. Jacobs had first suggested it. Recovery was supposed to be painful, and success rates weren't overwhelmingly good.

"It is an option we can pursue," said Dr. Jacobs.

"And the med board will withhold ruling until you've had time to recover and been reassessed," said Captain McLeod.

"Then let's do it," said Jonathan. "If it's my best option to stay in the Air Force, I have to try it."

TEN

HERE THEY SAT IN THE emergency room again. Lori had never suspected what the pneumonia a year and a half ago would do to her little boy's lungs. Of course, back then, with Jonathan deployed to the other side of the world and two little ones at home, she was just trying to survive the illness with her sanity intact. Now, with emergency room visits three other times during the summer plus the follow-up appointments with the pediatrician, on top of the regular well baby appointments for Austin and a routine appointment for Kay, she was getting to know the medics around the Malmstrom Clinic by name. She wasn't sure that was a good thing.

"Okay, mom," said the airman she knew as Tim. He usually had a good repartee with Charlie, but today Charlie wasn't feeling good enough to respond. She was so thankful that Jonathan could be home for this so she didn't have to worry about Kay and Austin in this crowded place as well as Charlie.

"His O₂ level is registering around ninety-two percent. Not great, but not as low as I was expecting, considering his demeanor. I'm going to go ahead and start some liquid albuterol until the doc can get over here."

"Thanks, Tim. I noticed you guys were busier than usual today."

"I'm not sure what to blame it on, but the drop in temperatures over the weekend and the full moon last night are both under suspicion." He winked at her as he worked. "Either way, the docs have been kept plenty busy, that's for sure."

Tim adjusted the oxygen mask around Charlie's face. "Can you hold this for me, buddy?" Charlie barely registered that Tim had spoken.

Nibbling on the inside of her cheek, Lori moved over to the bed and supported the canister.

"It should just take a few minutes, then you can release your hold. You know what to watch for?"

"Yes," said Lori. "I can hear the difference when the medicine is gone."

"Perfect. Doc Richardson will be here as quick as he can."

Lori brushed her hand over Charlie's cheek. "Try to take a good deep breath, buddy. The more you breathe in the medicine, the better you'll feel." Charlie stared out the gap in the curtain, watching the people scurry about without following any of their movements. Lori worried about his lack of response. *Please God*, she prayed, *let this medicine get deep into his lungs and make a difference quickly.*

After a few minutes, Lori heard the change in the airflow through the mask that signaled the albuterol was gone. She waited a few more minutes, hoping for someone to come back in to check on them. But when no one did, she walked over to the wall behind the bed to turn the flow of oxygen off and removed the mask from Charlie's face. Sitting down with him on the bed, he turned and curled up against her.

She wrapped her arm around him. "How are you feeling, buddy?"

He wrapped an arm around her. "Milk?"

The first food of any sort he'd asked for all day. She would take it as a positive sign that this was turning around. She got up to get the sippy cup she'd brought with them and handed it to him. "It's not milk, bud. It's juice."

He looked at her before taking a small drink and tucking the cup under his arm. He rolled over, laying his head on the small pillow covered in teddy bears that he carried with him everywhere they went.

"How's it going in here?" Tim asked, walking over to the monitors and checking Charlie's numbers.

"A little better, I think," said Lori. "He finally asked for something to drink."

"That's good. Let me have your hand, kiddo." Tim held Charlie's small hand in his, fastening the oxygen sensor to his middle finger. "Did he drink much?"

"No," Lori shook her head.

"Well, it's a start."

"What's his oxygen saturation at now?"

The brusque question took Lori by surprise. She turned to see a man in green scrubs standing just inside the opening in the curtains.

"About ninety-five," said Tim.

"Good." The man reached out a hand to Lori. "I'm Dr. Richardson. You told the medic that the whole family is sick with colds?"

Lori nodded. "Charlie's started a couple weeks ago, mostly with just some congestion, although he'd start coughing if he got running around much. We saw our pediatrician then, but he was doing okay. She told me just to watch him. He seemed to be struggling a little bit yesterday, but it really got worse overnight. I gave him some albuterol as soon as he woke up this morning, but that didn't seem to make a difference."

"Gotcha. So you have a nebulizer at home?"

Lori nodded.

"And what time was the dose you gave him this morning?"

Lori looked at her watch. "About two hours ago."

"Okay. I don't really want him to hang out here with all the flu cases we're seeing. That could exacerbate things quickly for him. Let's get him home and comfortable for now, keeping up the nebulizer treatments. If he takes another downturn, bring him back to us. Otherwise, follow up with his pediatrician tomorrow."

ANOTHER DAY, ANOTHER DOCTOR. With three young children and all of Jonathan's medical issues, Lori felt as if she was constantly either going to an appointment or waiting on results. She was getting pretty good at it all, but today, she couldn't watch. She turned her head as the doctor began pulling gauze from Jonathan's nose.

His commander had won the battle over his certification to work with nuclear weapons last month when the board had ruled to permanently decertify Jonathan due to his sleep apnea and insomnia. In order to gain recertification, Jonathan had volunteered for uvulopharyngealpalatoplasty with tonsillectomy, according to the follow-up appointment paper in her hand.

She couldn't say it even when she looked at it, but the best she understood, it meant the removal of his tonsils, adenoids, uvula, turbinate bones, and parts of his soft palate while repairing his pharynx. Surgery had been slightly longer than anticipated, but the doctors had been pleased. More practically, it meant that the back of his throat looked like raw ground meat, and he'd had to work hard to swallow antibiotic and pain pills every four hours. Not even Jell-O made them go down easy.

Today, they were back to have the doctor remove the packing from his nose and see how things were healing. Lori shifted Charlie on her hip and patted Kay's back. Her daughter didn't like looking at the bloody gauze any more than she did, and Kay had her head buried in Lori's hip. Lori couldn't believe the man was still pulling on the long strand. Exactly how much could they fit up in a person's nasal cavities?

"Is swallowing getting easier?" the doctor asked.

"A bit," said Jonathan. "I thought I'd never get those pills down the first evening I was home. Took about forty-five minutes, and I think I dissolved them in my mouth more than actually swallowed the pills."

"The first twenty-four hours are the roughest." The doctor was distracted for a moment while looking up Jonathan's nose. "Just a little more."

Finally, Lori saw him step away from Jonathan to dump all the gauze into the medical trash receptacle.

"Now, how does that feel?"

"Much better."

"We do pack it pretty tight up there. You will still be tender for several days, and I want you to be very cautious for at least another week. No horseplay with the kids or anything that could bang against your face. Say *ahh* for me."

He pointed a light down Jonathan's throat. "Well, everything looks good. I don't see anything we need to worry about or keep a close eye on. I want to see you again in one week, then probably two weeks after that. We'll give it four to six weeks total to heal, and then look at scheduling you for another sleep study. Hopefully this makes a significant difference for you."

"Sounds great."

Lori watched Jonathan gently touch his nose. It might have been the most tender movement she'd ever seen him make.

"You'll need to be careful when you eat. You don't have anything to encourage food to go down your throat anymore, so if you're not cognizant of how you're swallowing, food particles could go up into your nose instead of down your esophagus. Other than that, if you have any questions or concerns before your next appointment, give us a call."

"I will." Jonathan extended his hand to the doctor, who briefly shook it. "Thanks, doctor."

The doctor left, and Jonathan stood from where he'd been sitting on the medical table. "Ready to go?"

Lori nodded. "Doing okay?"

Jonathan grabbed the car seat with a sleeping Austin in it and held out his other hand for Kay to grab before they walked down the hall together. "I couldn't believe how much gauze they pulled out. I thought he would never stop."

"Daddy, that was gross!" said Kay.

Lori giggled. "It was pretty disgusting."

Jonathan crouched down to look Kay in the eye. "You were very good in there while you were waiting for me."

Kay smiled broadly at Jonathan. Lori soaked in the sight of her husband and daughter, totally absorbed in each other for the brief moment. Her heart warmed, and she hugged Charlie tighter.

"How about," said Jonathan, "we stop for an ice cream cone on the way home."

"Yes!" said Kay, launching both her arms high in the air before jumping and throwing herself at her daddy.

Lori laughed. "It's November!"

"So?" said Jonathan.

"It's ice cream!" said Kay. "Charlie, you want some ice cream?"

Charlie nodded as Lori shook her head. "You guys are crazy."

Jonathan lifted Kay as he stood and pulled them all in close. "It's never too cold for ice cream."

Lori looked at him. "It's almost always too cold for ice cream."

Jonathan smiled and leaned in close to Kay's face. "Mommy's the crazy one."

Kay agreed. "Yeah, Momma. You crazy."

ONCE AGAIN, JONATHAN sat across from Captain McLeod, his ever-expanding medical file open before them.

"So, the notes I received late last week said surgery went well and healing is progressing as expected."

"Yes, sir," said Jonathan. "I return next week for my three-week follow-up. In December, we'll begin talking about when we should schedule my next sleep study."

"Very good." The captain sat back in his chair. "Anything else we need to discuss?"

Jonathan didn't want to mention quite yet that Lori had said his snoring seemed worse. He wouldn't raise that concern until the sleep study confirmed it. Besides, he was hoping it would ease up as his nose continued to heal and the crusting from where his turbinates had been cut ceased.

But, he would share one other idea that had come to him while reading through his medical records. "I do have one concern. I was reading the reports from my sleep studies more closely, and I saw that one doctor felt my insomnia was psychophysiological. I've seen lots of doctors trying to get a better handle on the physical aspects of this, but I'm not confident that the psychological aspects have been addressed yet."

Captain McLeod sat up and pulled the file closer to him. Flipping through several pages, he asked, "Do you remember which report that was on?"

"I believe it was the last one from the sleep clinic."

Jonathan waited as the captain read through a few pages. "Yes, here it is." He read for another moment. "Hmm. I see what you mean. Well, I can schedule an appointment for you with mental health as soon as I get back to my desk. It's worth checking, just in case that might help solve some of the issues."

"Thank you, sir. I appreciate that." Jonathan figured it was a long shot, but he didn't want to walk away from this with any doubts that he had done everything possible.

"Okay. So, I'll let you know when that's scheduled, and we'll plan to meet about a week after that appointment. Sound good?"

"Yes, sir. Thank you."

They stood and shook hands. "I'll be in touch."

ELEVEN

IT HAD BEEN THREE WEEKS since Jonathan had last sat in this room that was becoming all too familiar. Now, as he waited for Captain McLeod to join him, he paced by the window overlooking the parking lot. He couldn't see much else, since this side of the base faced the Midwestern plains. Wheat fields and more wheat fields stretched out between where he stood and the metropolis of Billings. Well, that was an overstatement, but compared to Great Falls, Billings felt like a sprawling metropolis.

Captain McLeod rushed in, shutting the door behind him. "Sorry to keep you waiting." He assumed his usual seat at the head of the table as Jonathan took his normal place to the man's left. "I was on the phone with the psychiatrist you saw over at mental health."

"Was he more encouraging to you than he was to me?"

The captain paused from shuffling through his papers. "What did he tell you?"

"That insomnia is often related to associations between the bed and sleep difficulties, so until we get everything else straightened out and my stress reduced, any psychological treatment would be ineffective."

"Did he actually say that, or was that your impression from what all he said?"

"That last part is pretty much a word-for-word quote."

"Well," said Captain McLeod. He leaned back in his chair. "What do you think now?"

"I think a lot is riding on this next sleep study, but I'm not optimistic. Of course, my wife would tell you that I'm not normally optimistic about anything."

Captain McLeod smiled. "Glass is usually half empty, huh?"

Jonathan nodded. "And someone's about to come drink that."

The captain laughed. "That's good. My wife would probably say my outlook is pretty similar. That might be one of the reasons why I've been fighting so hard for you."

Jonathan wanted to keep fighting, but he no longer cared about staying in a nuclear weapons security detail or proving his commander wrong. Truthfully, he and God had been having a lot of discussions. Well, Jonathan had been talking a bunch anyway. If he was really honest, he had to admit that God had asked a question, and he had been avoiding answering it while he rambled on about everyone else.

"I see your sleep study is scheduled for right after Christmas."

Jonathan nodded.

God whispered. "Well? Ready to do it My way?"

Jonathan squirmed.

"The medical board is scheduled to meet again on your case mid-January. That will give me time to get the report from the doctors and add it to your file."

"Here's the thing." Jonathan paused. Could he really do this? "I'll keep my appointment with the sleep study clinic, of course. I at least need to get my CPAP air pressure adjusted because it's set too high now that I've had my surgery. It chokes me every time I try to use it."

"Okay. But why do I feel like you're changing horses on me?"

"I still want to stay in the Air Force. That hasn't changed at all. But, I'm thinking my career needs to change if I'm going to be an effective troop. My commander isn't going to change his mind, and my medical history is going to limit my worldwide qualifications. We can't fix either one of those, no matter what the sleep study determines."

"Are you saying you want to pursue retraining?"

"Do you have a better idea? My commander, permanent decertification, and possible separation from active duty have been significant stressors for months. I can't keep moving in that and expect my sleep to improve. And if my sleep doesn't improve, I can't expect to be recertified."

"I follow you." A moment passed before the captain said anything else. "It's a sound argument, and I think I agree with you. But what does your wife say? If you're approved, it will mean at least one move within the next year, maybe two depending on how long it takes them to approve this and how long your school is."

Jonathan smiled, confident in Lori's ability to handle the upcoming changes. "She's always up for a new adventure. Plus, she can't wait to get out of Montana."

"Any idea what occupational specialty you want to retrain into?"

Jonathan didn't hesitate. It had been a developing passion before he joined the Air Force, but he didn't have the confidence back then to think he could be good at it. Back then, he'd gone with the safer path, but that had brought lots of heartache. Now he knew his passion back then had been God's plan all along. He was just too stubborn to take a chance on it. He wouldn't repeat that mistake. "Computers. I want to retrain into Information Technologies."

The captain nodded. "All right. Let me grab the right form from my files, and we'll get it submitted."

LORI SAT IN HER GLIDER in the living room with only the lights from the Christmas tree shining. It was a beautiful tree, even if she did have to make sure a couple of the artificial branches were propped just so. This year, the holidays were so different from the year before, and she felt some of the hope and joy she'd once had about all things December returning to her again.

Oh, life wasn't perfect. Jonathan still struggled to sleep, and they were waiting to see if his request for retraining would be approved or if the medical board would discharge them. Every once in a while, unanswered questions would swirl through her heart and mind, but not often. Most days, she could turn the worries off. She knew God was in control, and she relied on it. She even repeated that truth to herself when she fought the doubts. She prayed for answers, she prayed for peace to cover Jonathan, and she prayed for her children being raised in this nomadic lifestyle. So much uncertainty surrounded them, but she would let God be her fortress and lead her family to do the same.

"Momma!" Kay ran into the room and crashed into her,

which startled Austin, who was sitting in his walker nearby playing with a few soft, plastic animals from a Noah's Ark set.

"Kay!" Lori smiled at her bundle of energy. Her precious daughter who loved dresses and bows but would probably always give her brothers a run for their money.

"Can we watch *Rudolph*? Will you turn it on for us and come watch it with us?"

Lori cupped Kay's face, rubbing her thumb over her cheek. "Did you leave Charlie downstairs?" Little feet pattering near the top of the stairs answered her question.

"I told him to stay, Momma. I did. I told Charlie to wait for me and I would ask."

Lori laughed. She looked at the clock noting that it was almost time to put the kids to bed. Jonathan was back in their bedroom, strumming on his guitar, and as much as part of her enjoyed the quiet of a few minutes ago, most of her looked forward to some simple Christmas magic with her kids. *Rudolph* sounded wonderful. "Do you think Daddy will want to watch it with us?"

Charlie came running in, crashing into her chair much like Kay had. "Rudolph? Watch Rudolph?"

"Charlie!" yelled Kay. "Let's go ask Daddy if he wants to watch too!"

As the two went charging down the hallway to plow into Jonathan, Lori walked over to pull Austin from his chair. "I think it's time we introduce you to our favorite reindeer." She nestled him close, listening to the chatter from the back of the house.

It was going to be a great Christmas.

AUTHOR'S EPILOGUE

THANK YOU FOR JOINING me for this journey with a real-life family. Yes, Jonathan, Lori, Kay, Charlie, and Austin are real, although their names have been changed to protect their identities. Their struggles in Montana were also real, as was the commander who shared a name with the bad guy from one of Lori's favorite movie series and who didn't believe the diagnoses Jonathan received from multiple doctors.

In the December 2002 sleep study, Jonathan received news that surgery had made his sleep apnea worse. As a result, his permanent decertification to work around nuclear weapons was confirmed. In February 2003, Jonathan's commander wrote a letter to the medical board recommending medical separation. However, the Senior Master Sergeant that Jonathan worked for at the job watching over the dorm rooms for unaccompanied airman wrote a letter to the board stating, "There is no reason in the world to medically separate this individual. The medical condition is only treated at night while he is sleeping. I highly recommend this outstanding NCO be given the opportunity to continue serving his country." The board approved Jonathan's continued service with the United States Air Force, and later that year he was approved for retraining into Communications.

After more medical issues came to light and after months of additional testing, the man you know as Jonathan once again submitted to a med board. He asked for medical retirement, which they granted in July 2008. He now continues to serve his country with the civil service in the Department of the Army.

Lori, Kay, Charlie, and Austin supported Jonathan through several more moves, including his second tech school in Mississippi, a duty station in North Carolina, and civil service jobs in North Carolina and Virginia.

Lori discovered God had bigger plans for her than she'd ever dreamed. Still an introvert, she loves to spend time with military spouses and challenge them to thrive where God has them, even when it's not comfortable.

Kay didn't always like God's plan, and one move in particular sticks out in her mind that was harder than all the rest. But she discovered for herself that God has a plan that is always good. Now she walks forward, seeking God's purpose as she launches out on her own.

Soon after the end of our story, Charlie was diagnosed with asthma and suffered many attacks throughout his childhood, including more emergency room visits than Lori can remember and two separate multiple-day hospital stays. The move to the Eastern United States helped his eczema, and he was able to leave the careful care of his dry skin behind. As he grew, his asthma attacks gradually occurred less, becoming more of a seasonal concern. Eventually, they left him entirely, and his doctor has declared that he's outgrown his asthma.

Austin grew up as the stereotypical baby of the family, loved by both his siblings, at least until he got old enough to annoy Charlie more than he helped him. As his siblings find their way on their own, he pays attention and tries to learn from their mistakes so he doesn't have to repeat them.

DID YOU LIKE THIS BOOK?

Would you please leave a review with your favorite bookstore or book club?

Want more from Carrie Daws? Check out all the book related Freebies available at CarrieDaws.com. You'll find book club discussion guides, other books in the series, and more!

Want even more? Carrie loves to support and talk with Christian readers! Not only does she personally respond to every email she receives, but she writes weekly devotions based on themes within her books. Check it out on CarrieDaws.com!

ABOUT THE AUTHOR

GOD REWROTE CARRIE'S dreams from being a corporate accountant to an author. With a background writing devotions, a mentor encouraged her to think bigger. The writing monster she now barely keeps contained was born.

After ten years in the US Air Force, Carrie's husband medically retired, and they settled in North Carolina. With their three children figuring out what they want to do in life after high school, Carrie stays busy keeping up with her family, loving on women, and reading as much as she can.

ALSO BY CARRIE DAWS

THE CROSSING SERIES
Crossing Values

Ryan's Crossing

Romancing Melody

Crossing's Redemption

THE EMBERS SERIES
Kindling Embers

Igniting Embers

Extinguishing Embers

THE SACRED TRUST SERIES
Seeking Isabel

Finding Benjamin

Banishing Felipe

HOME FRONT HEROINES
More Than Meets the Eye

Not My Ways

www.ingramcontent.com/pod-product-compliance
Lightning Source LLC
Chambersburg PA
CBHW020415130626
46549CB00006B/2565